Unhappy Home
-Written By-
Envy Mayes and Linette King

Copyright © 2016 by True Glory
Publications
Published by True Glory Publications
Join our Mailing List by texting True
Glory to 99000 or click here
http://optin.mobiniti.com/V2Y

Facebook: **Author Linette King and Envy Mayes**

Cover Design: Tina Louise
Editor: Tamyra L. Griffin

Table of Contents

Jaquan
Kareem
Miko

Acknowledgements

Linette King: First off and foremost I have to give thanks to God who is the head of my household and my life for without him, I am nothing. **To my children:** Aaliyah, Alannah and Jaye, I love you guys so much and everything that I do is for you. Remember to always follow your dreams and never ever limit yourself. I want nothing short of the best for you and for you to reach your brain's full potential and be great. **To the readers:** I know this took forever to be released and it's mostly my fault because I am the worst procrastinator in the world, but I hope you enjoy this exciting read! **Erica:** Writing this book with you has been so fun! I love you girl!

Envy Mayes: I give honor and praise to God for guiding my steps through this journey. **To my children:** I love you to pieces. Jovont'a and Martavious, Rest In Peace. Not a day goes by that I don't think about y'all and miss you like crazy. Quadarius and Savion, the sky's the limit and no one can hold you down. Never give up on your dreams, even the ones others think are silly. All things are possible if you just believe in yourself and remember, I got your back. Destiny and Shanequa, I have watched you grow into beautiful strong women right before my eyes. Y'all are bossy, ambitious and fearless. Hell, when you're together, you give me strength. My kids are the best of me! **To my readers:** I adore you and cherish your support. You all make it worth it. To one of the most amazing people in the world, **Linette King**, thank you for giving me this opportunity to work with you. You are a joy, love you for life.

Make sure you read this all the way to the end for sneak peeks from both authors!!!! You don't want to miss what's next!!!

Nakia

"We moving in two weeks, so have your things packed and ready to go." my mom said to me. It was the middle of the school year, I didn't want to move! Plus, I have a crush on someone that I wasn't ready to let go of. I didn't say anything though because when my mom made up her mind to do something, she did it regardless of how you felt.

On my last day of school, I stood outside and hugged my friends as I told them goodbye. Jaquan approached me and asked if he could speak to me in private.

"Ooh you go bitch! Get your man!" my silly friend Renee clowned me. I was so embarrassed and all I could do was shake my head as he pulled me to the side.

"Nakia, I heard that you were leaving and I just wanted to say goodbye." he said. He stared at me for a few seconds then gave me a hug. "I really am going to miss you lil Mama." Jaquan confessed. My heart fluttered with excitement and my mouth got dry.

'Ask your questions now are forever hold your peace.' I thought to myself. Nothing about me says peace, so I fired off questions. "Are you?" I asked.

"Yes I am." he answered with a smile.

"Well you know I been had a crush on you for a while and I thought you liked me too; so why you never approached me?" I asked.

He smiled at me with the most beautiful smile and my heart melted. "I do like you. Maybe a little more than I should like you but you know I have a girlfriend. I may be many things but a cheater I'm not." Jaquan said honestly.

He gave me another hug and kiss on the cheek before he walked away. We lost contact with each other for about five years. Until we bumped into each other again at a friend's birthday party. I saw him as soon as he walked in.

"Damn, milk does the body good! That joker is fine as hell!" I exclaimed. *'Nakia! Pull yourself together girl. You are not single and with looks like that he probably ain't either.'* I coached myself as I giggled.

I took another sip of my drink just as my friends Shiwana and Kenna came rushing towards me all excited and shit. They told me who all was there from high school, how good they look, and how they had come up. I knew these hoes were about to get long winded.

"Let's sit down on the couch over there, my feet hurt." I suggested.

We had fun catching up and talking about the good old days until the DJ got on the mic.

"I want everybody to stand to your feet and get your grown folk on as we bring the man of the hour to the stage, Christian Carter!" The room applauded as he walked to the mic.

"I would like to thank everybody for coming out to share this special occasion with me." he said. "Looking out in the crowd I see a lot of my old classmates from Columbia High in the building." he paused then looked around some more. "Go Eagles!" he cheered. Cheers and whistles erupted from the crowd as he continued to speak.

"I would like to thank my mom and my beautiful fiance for putting this all together for me." he said. "My mom couldn't make it tonight but baby, come on up here and a take a bow." he said to his fiance. "This party is hot, don't y'all agree?" he yelled as we waited for her to make her way to the stage.

"YESSSS!" we yelled our response.

The party really was on point and the setup was amazing. "A lot of you may remember her from High School, Ms. Miko Grey." he said.

"Wait, what?" I damn near choked. *'It has to be a different Miko Grey.'* I thought to myself; but when she walked out on that stage, glowing like a ray of sunshine, all of my doubts were confirmed. It was her.

My eyes went straight across the room to where I had seen Jaquan standing a few minutes ago. Sure enough he was standing there with a look of shock and disbelief. Miko was the girlfriend that Jaquan had been with for the longest. She was the bitch that stood in between my happily ever after. To see her now standing on stage pregnant and engaged to one of his closest friends had me heated. When I saw him storm out of the club I ran after him. By the time I made it outside he was at the bottom step.

"Wait! Wait Jaquan!!" I screamed as I waved my hand in the air to get his attention.

"Who is that?" he asked as he turned back around towards the steps.

I had taken my heels off so I could run down the steps. I took them two at a time until I stood face to face with him. "It's me." I said completely out of breath.

"Nakia?" he questioned with his eyes bucked wide. "Man, it's been a long time lil mama and you still looking better than ever." he said.
"One could say the same about you." I replied with a seductive grin.

We both stood there staring into each other eyes for a brief moment not knowing what to say. After all, it had been years since we talked or seen each other. I decided to be the one to break the ice on this awkward situation.

"Listen, I saw the hurt on your face when Christian made his announcement tonight.

I just wanted to make sure you were okay." I confessed.

"Aww, you still a good friend I see." he said. He brushed his finger across my chin. "Well thanks for your concern. I really appreciate it but right now I need to be alone to wrap my mind around this shit." he stated. He handed me a card with his number on it and told me to call him the following day. "We should have lunch and catch up." he said then walked away and headed down the sidewalk.

My heart was telling me to run behind him, but my mind was saying to just let him go. I followed my mind, but I also pulled out my cell phone and dialed the number on the card. "Hello?" he answered.

"Hey it's Nakia; this is my number." I said nervously.

"Okay shawty I'm locking you in now." he replied and I hung up the phone.

I didn't really feel up to partying no more so I sent Shiwana and Makenna a text saying I was going home.

As I walked to my car, I couldn't help but think about how good things were when all of us was younger. I thought about all of the bad and illegal shit we did trying to fit in. Things like egging cars, stealing candy from the corner store, and playing pranks on the teachers. I shook my head because we were a mess. One thing I will never forget is how Juquan would look out for all of us though; especially for Christian and Jeremiah Carter. I remember Jaquan and his cousins getting into countless fights taking up for them.

When we were like in the eighth grade, their mom Ms. Betsy lost her job and started drinking a lot. Jaquan would take his extra money and buy them food. He stole them clothes and everything. *'Wow, and to betrayed like that; I can't imagine how he feels.'* I thought to myself.

'I just wanted to love all his problems away.' I thought as I pulled into my sister's driveway to pick up my daughter Amberia. "Damn I guess what they say is true. Dont trust no one." I said out loud to myself.

<u>Jaquan</u>

I couldn't believe the woman I once loved was about to marry someone I considered my brother. Then to make matters worse, neither one of them had the decency to contact me to tell me. I spoke with Christian at least three times a week and Miko had just paid me a visit two weeks ago. The thought alone made me sick to my stomach and that's why I had to get away from Nakia fast. She looked so beautiful in her black, strapless dress. I checked her out completely from her freshly done hair to pedicured toes. I began to regret being loyal to Miko's ass and missing the opportunity to be with Nakia. When I gave her my card, I not only wanted her to have my number, I also wanted her to know that in a few years, I'd be able to take care of her.

I'd just started at a law firm and with hard work and dedication, I knew I would be great; because being great was my only option. Seeing Nakia was the highlight of my night though. The only bright spot that I could see.

Somehow as I walked to my car, my thoughts kept drifting back off to my cousin Christian, who was more like a brother to me, and my trifling ex-girlfriend Miko. What the two of them has done is unforgivable. My thoughts drifted back to my encounter with Miko just two short weeks ago.

"Jay Miller." I answered my desk phone as I continued to sort through my case files. I'd

asked to prove myself and Mr. Bowers gave me a load of cases to get started on; twelve cases to be exact, so I knew I'd be hella busy for a while.

"Hey Quan. I need to see you." Miko cooed over the phone.

I sighed because I knew exactly what she wanted but I was a man on a mission. The last thing I was thinking about was pussy and that's the very reason that we broke up. Miko had it in her mind that since I wasn't giving it to her then I had to be giving it to somebody; but the truth of that matter is, I was broke and I couldn't get horny broke. Hell, I couldn't sleep peacefully broke. I couldn't do anything broke but focus on getting money.

"I'm a little busy right now." I responded to her only for her to suck her teeth. She never understood that I had dreams. I needed a woman with vision and I knew she wasn't that woman so when she broke up with me, I didn't try at all to get her back.

"You still putting me last." she whined into the phone as if we were still together.

We hadn't had sex in months and I know I was wrong for neglecting her but when we got rich I knew I would pipe it to her every chance I got.
"Miko, you know that isn't the case." I tried to explain but she cut me off.

"I'll be by when you get off," she said and hung the phone up before I had a chance to respond. I just shook my head and continue to go through the cases.

My job was to treat each case as if I was the lawyer fighting to get the client off and present it to Mr. Bowers. They were each set to go to trial in exactly three weeks, so I needed to get all of my ducks in a row so Mr. Bowers wouldn't look like an ass in the end.

By the end of my work day, I was beyond hungry. I'd worked straight through my lunch break for the second day in a row and all I wanted to do was bite into a juicy super-sonic double bacon cheeseburger, take a shower and go to bed.

I left work, went straight to Sonic's and ate my food on the way home. I'd completely forgotten about Miko dropping by until I saw her car parked in the driveway of my two-bedroom home. I pinched the bridge of my nose and prepared myself for an argument that I didn't want to have. That was another thing that I had grown tired of. Whenever she didn't get her way, she would pick a fight and disappear for days, sometimes weeks.

I got out and walked inside of my house only to hear slow music playing. I was tired and I still didn't want to have sex with her. We were damn near at the point of no return, but I still had love for her.

"We need to talk." I said as soon as I walked through my room door.

I looked up and saw her completely naked on my bed with a sexy little frown on her face. I was too tired to fuck but I knew my dick wasn't as it strained against the zipper of my slacks.
"Later."

She smirked once she saw how hard my dick was. It was crazy how you could fuck the attitude right out of Miko at any given moment.

She crawled off the bed and walked over to me as her nipples stared me in my eyes. I leaned over slightly and took one of them nipples in my mouth as I twirled the other one between my fingers. Miko simultaneously unbuckled my belt and pants, then pulled my dick out so fast that I didn't realize her nipple wasn't in my mouth anymore until I was balls deep in her mouth. She hummed loudly as she deep throated me. My toes threw up gang signs as she massaged my balls along with the soft vibrations from the back of her throat and light suction. Shit damn near drove me crazy.

She sucked, hummed and moaned as I tried desperately to keep my balance. About a minute or so later, she had done swallowed all of my nut and licked my dick clean. She was nasty like that, but I loved every bit of it.

Miko stood to her feet, grabbed my hand and led me to the bed. I watched her climb up *first, sit on her knees and place her forehead on my comforter set. The sight of her neatly shaven pussy caused me to want to slide deep inside of her. I reached in my nightstand and grabbed a condom just as she reached back and opened her pussy wider for me. My mouth watered and I hadn't tasted her in so long that I ended up with my face buried in her pussy until she came all down my chin and neck. I smiled as I climbed on the bed behind her. SMACK! I gave her ass a loud smack then eased into her. She moaned and began to throw it in a circle.*

BEEEEEEEEEEP!!!!!

The sound of a horn being blown behind me brought me back to reality. I had done got in my car and drove away from the club without even realizing it because I was so deep in thought. I looked down at my lap and shook my head at my hard dick.

"You won't be experiencing anything like that anytime soon." I broke the news to him as I drove away from the traffic light.

My thoughts drifted back to the announcement that Christian made at the club. He'd mentioned his chick plenty of times, but not one time did he ever say her name. I was in a state of shock once again as I made my way home. I needed to smoke me a big blunt when I got there so I could clear my mind and continue to work on my cases. I planned to do any and everything I could to keep my mind busy and off the betrayal of my brother and ex-girlfriend.

Nakia

"Wake up sis." my sister Candace said as she shook me awake. I groaned and tried to turn over but she didn't leave me alone.

"Man gone before I chop you in your neck." I said as I tried to push her away. One thing I hated was for people to wake me up, and she knew that! She just didn't give a damn.

"Ssh.. Hush before you wake the kids up. My baby daddy left us some lemon skunk to smoke." she said with a knowing grin plastered across her face.

"You lying!" I exclaimed and sat up with my body filled with excitement. There was no better weed to smoke than lemon skunk and I couldn't wait to take a pull of it.

"No I'm not; follow me to the patio." she responded then walked out of the room.

"Ugh!" I groaned slowly as I got out of the bed.

This heifer get on my nerves. I know I should have taken my ass home last night. Hell, I only stay around the corner; but it's all good. I actually did more tossing and turning than I did sleeping anyway.

I got up and threw on a pair of leggings and some slides. I grabbed my phone then went to join Candace on the patio. The view was beautiful and so peaceful that I could actually hear the birds chirping as she fired up the blunt.

"So how was the party last night?" she asked. I smirked at her as I reflected briefly on my luck.

"Funny you should ask." I began then closed my eyes. "Because it was very interesting." I continued with one eye slightly open. She raised an eyebrow so I knew I'd piqued her interest.

"How so?" Candace asked as she passed the blunt to me.

"Well first, guess who I saw." I said as I slid to the edge of my chair. I took a deep pull from the blunt.

"Who?" she asked as she rotated the chair so she was facing me.

I choked on the weed a little bit because it was strong. Then my lips formed a straight line as I waited for her to guess.

"Girl just tell me! It's too early in the morning to be playing the guessing game." she stated clearly annoyed. I stared at her for several more seconds.

"Alright damn! With your moody ass." I mocked her attitude playfully as I rolled my eyes. "Jaquan Miller." I admitted with a sly smile.

"Are you serious? Your first love was there at the party?" she asked with her voice laced with excitement.

"Yes; and sis he was looking extremely good!" I said to her as I pinched my legs closed tightly together. Just thinking about him had my pussy playing games.

"So what happened? You can't just leave me hanging like that." she complained with her nosey ass.

"He wasn't much for socializing after Christan announced that him and Miko were getting married." I said to her as I shook my head.

"What?!" Candace damn near screamed. Her mouth was wide open just like mines when I'd heard it. "Nakia!" she dragged my name out. "No they did not do Jaquan like that after all he did for both of them." Her mouth hung wide open in disbelief. "Damn sis I need a drink after this." Candace claimed.

"Girl it's seven-thirty in the morning and you talking about drinking." I said as I shook my head. She ignored me and walked back inside of the house.

"While you in there fix me one too." I called out to her and we both burst out laughing. She came back with two vodka and cranberry juices then sat them on the table.

"Well did you at least get his number or give him yours?" she asked after she took a sip from her glass and took a seat.

"Yes I did nosey and he wants to have lunch today; but I don't think I'm going." I admitted.

"Oh bitch you going!!" she said without looking up from her phone.

"To be honest, I'm not trying to add no more drama than I already have dealing with Kareem." I confessed sadly.

Kareem, also known as Casamoney, is my boyfriend and Amberia's daddy. Lately our relationship has been rocky because he won't keep his dick in his pants and is always out of town on so called business. It really bothered me that I couldn't trust him.

"This the nigga you worried about right here?" Candace asked as she handed her phone over to me.

I grabbed the phone and instantly, my body filled with anger as I stared at pictures of him on Instagram hugged up with another bitch.

"He got me fucked up!" I said with my free hand covering my mouth.

They were popping bottles and everything; looking very acquainted like he didn't have a family at home. I couldn't even lie or pretend like it didn't bother me because that shit hurt me to the core. If Jaquan felt anything like this last night, he'd need a friend and so do I.

I didn't want my sister to see me cry so I picked up my glass and phone then went back in the room and closed the door. A few minutes later, I heard my sister close the patio door and walk down the hall.

"That nigga is not worth your tears sis." she said from the door. "Listen out for the kids I need to run to the store and get some breakfast." she stated before she walked away.

Thank God she left because I really wanted to be left alone to drown in my sorrows with tears rolling down my face. I called the one person I knew I could trust, Jaquan. I knew it was early as hell, but my heart was hurting and I needed him. On the third ring he answered.

"Hello?" he said in the sexiest sleep filled voice I'd ever heard.

"Jaquan." I managed to get out before the flood came. I opened my mouth so I could keep talking but only more sobs escaped.

"Nakia? What's wrong baby?" he asked but it only made me cry harder. "Are you hurt?" he asked a voice filled with concern.

"Just my feelings." I finally blurted out. After all of these years of Kareem and I being together he's hurt me so much, so I didn't understand why it still hurt me so bad.

"Talk to me. Tell me what happened." he said in a sympathetic tone.

I broke down and told him everything I had been going thru for the last three years. Even down to the fact of him having outside kids while we were together. We talked on the phone for a while and agreed to meet up at the Olive Garden today at one o'clock.

"Okay, I will see you later." I cooed then hung up the phone.

The smell of bacon and pancakes tickled my nose as my stomach growled. I got up and went to help my sister make breakfast, but when I got to the kitchen she was already done and fixing plates. I giggled to myself a little because she was just like our mom, who always hummed in the kitchen as she cooked. "Kids come eat!" she yelled. They sounded like a herd of cattle running down the steps, so I politely stepped to the side to avoid getting knocked down. When it came down to eating, our kids were the truth.

"Sis come grab a seat, I cooked enough for you too." Candace said. I knew this was just an attempt to get in my business but what the hell, I was hungry. "So what time is your date?" Candace asked with a cheesy smile plastered on her face.

"What makes you think I have a date?" I asked as I bit a piece of bacon.

"Girl please! You have always loved Jaquan and now that you both are going thru some heartbreak, it's only right that y'all be there for each other." Candace spat out with a slight shrug of her shoulders.

"I will keep my niecey pooh; you go get yourself together and enjoy your day." she said with a smile.

I picked up my daughter so I could love on her before I left. Amberia is my life and I loved her to pieces.

Later on that day....The Date

As soon as I walked in the door of Olive Garden I saw Jaquan sitting at the bar. *'Oh my God, he looked better than he did last night.'* I thought to myself as I took in his attire. He was dressed in some tan slacks and a peach colored shirt that fit his 6'1" frame just perfectly. He got up to greet me with a hug. He smelled so good and I felt so safe in his arms. The Hostess came over to seat us; we ordered our food and some drinks and waited.

We were having such a good time reminiscing and talking about our crazy situtationships. I hadn't laughed like that in a while and it felt good. Just being in the presence of a real man had me floating on cloud 9.

"Bitch you got me fucked up!!!" I heard a loud voice yell from behind me.

Before I could turn around good, Casamoney and his homeboy were standing in front of us. He attempted to grab me, but was stopped in his tracks by Jaquan.

Jaquan

I've never been one to raise my hand to hit a woman so I'd be damn if any nigga was about to hit one in front of me. I saw Kareem's punk ass as soon as him and Mario walked through the doors. I knew it was going to be a problem but I knew it was nothing for me to solve it; so I didn't acknowledge him at all until he tried to grab Nakia. Now of course that wasn't something that I was going to go for.

See I knew all about Kareem's snitching ass because I work for one of the largest law firms ever. I specialize in criminal defense and right now, I'm trying to make a name for myself; and it just so happen that I came across his name last night as I reviewed one of my case files.

"This ain't got shit to do with you pretty boy!" Kareem snapped as he snatched away from me and took a step back. I shoved Nakia behind me softly as I stood toe to toe with her boyfriend and his friend.

"From the moment you came over here disrespecting her I been in it." I stated calmly as I looked directly in his eyes. I noticed he kept looking behind me at her, but I didn't know if she was looking at him or not.

We had drawn the attention of the other customers so I knew we'd be asked to leave soon if I couldn't de-escalate the situation. As crazy as it sounds, I didn't want to de-escalate it. From what she had told me, he couldn't get his shit together; so this is exactly what he needed to see. Most of the time, niggas dog you out because you let them. If you give them a taste of their medicine, they'll look at you differently. Nakia placed a trembling hand on my shoulder and to me, that only meant one thing, he'd been abusive.

"Bitch where the fuck is my baby while you out being a hoe?!" he ignored me and said to her.

I was beyond tired of him being disrespectful but an assault charge would ruin my career before it ever got started good. I had to think logically since we were out in public.

"She's safe." I said to him before Nakia could get a word out. I could tell by the way that he breathed heavily that he was going to fuck her up once he got her away from me.

"Grab your purse Nakia so we can go." I said and waited for her to reach over and grab it. He intercepted her and held the purse up in an extremely childish way. Mario chuckled until he noticed that I had turned my attention to him.

"Give me her purse so we can get out of here." I said calmly.

I could see a manager walking in our direction. His face was red as our waitress tailed him like they were on a mission to get us out before things got out of hand.

"Naw man." he said to me and I could tell she'd hurt his ego by the tone of his voice before he looked back at Nakia. "Man where my baby?" he asked her but by then Nakia had had enough.

She stepped around me and looked him dead in his eyes. "You have done nothing but hurt me over and over and you know what, I blamed myself. I thought something was wrong with me because I wasn't enough for you!." she snapped as she began to poke him in his chest with each word that came out of her mouth. "But you know what Kareem, fuck you and everything you stand for!" she yelled then snatched her purse out of his grasp just as the manager made it to us.

I was shocked at what she had just done and I could tell he was too as he stood before me with his mouth wide open.

"Do we have a problem here?" the manager asked but Nakia just walked away and headed out of the store.

"Sorry about that." I apologized to the manager then turned my attention back on Kareem.

"Close ya mouth playa." I said then walked off behind Nakia.

It wasn't until I heard Kareem cursing that I turned and realized I hadn't paid our tab. I found it quite comical that the manager made him pay for it.

"Are you okay?" I asked Nakia once I caught up with her.

She nodded her head but didn't turn away from what she was doing. I peeked around her to catch a glimpse just as she dropped her keys. Her hands were trembling as she reached down to pick them back up. I grabbed her hand and turned her around to face me. Her tear drenched face pissed me off immediately. That nigga didn't deserve her tears, but that isn't what she needed to hear. I could tell her that all day long, but I knew it wouldn't register. As a man, I knew I had to give her a reason not to cry.

I wiped her tears away then kissed her forehead softly. As much as I wanted to kiss her lips, I knew now wasn't the time. Shit if you ask me, sex is the cure to everything; even if the feeling of bliss is only temporary. At the same time, I knew she was hurting and us having sex would only complicate the situation.

"It's gone get better baby and I'm gonna take you from him." I said then kissed her on the forehead again.

She kept her eyes closed, more than likely trying to keep the tears at bay. I wanted to give her tough love, but if I tried that at this moment she'd pull away for sure and that's not what I wanted her to do.
"I don't know how much more of this I can take Quan. I'm so tired." she cried as she let her head hang low. I grabbed her and pulled her to me as she cried on my chest.

"Hey, remember when we were kids and you wanted to marry Prince?" I asked her.

She lifted her head off of me then looked at me with a confused look on her face but nodded her head.

"Yeah. I told you that you were just mad because you weren't sexy like him." she said as she used the back of her hand to wipe away her tears.

"Man you had me so jealous of that nigga. I used to go home singing in the mirror and shit man." I said and she started laughing. "Man you laughing and I'm serious! I had my shirt halfway open and some more shit!" I continued with a frown on my face.

"Man you lying." she said with a bright smile.

Her face was damn near dry so I knew I was on the right track and doing my job.

"Remember when I got my hair cut off after I grew it out for braids?" I asked because I was about to lay one on her.

"Yeah, you said it was time for you to be a man." she said with a slight smile on her face.

"Man I tried to perm my damn hair so it would look like his and it fell out." I replied honestly and she fell out laughing. Her sad tears had turned into tears of joy. *'Mission accomplished.'* I thought to myself as I watched her struggle to catch her breath.

I glanced back and saw Kareem and Mario walk out of the building. She didn't see him because she was bent over laughing hysterically. I shook my head at him, so he knew not to come this way on the bullshit.

"This ain't over." he mouthed to me.

"You right." I responded as I watched them walk off in the opposite direction.

"Man you laughing too hard now." I said to her with a deep frown on my face. I pretended to be upset but I was a little salty about her response to my truth.

"I'm sorry Quan; that just made my whole day though." she said as she stared at me. Her lip trembled and I could tell she was holding back her laughter.

"Go ahead Kia. Laugh at my pain then." I said and she fell out laughing again. It took her silly ass about ten minutes before she calmed down enough to get in her car.

"Thank you." she said once she was situated.
I didn't want our date to end but she had to handle her business and I had a shitload of cases I needed to go over, so it had to.

"Just call me if you need anything ma."
I said and she smiled.

I watched her drive away then made my
way home.

Kareem

"Damn man. I can't believe you let them play you like that." my boy Mario said as we walked to the car.

I opened the passenger's seat and climbed in as he walked around to the driver's side. My blood was boiling and this shit was far from over.

"Yeah, he gone get his." I said through gritted teeth as Mario backed his truck up.

I glared at the back of his head. Yeah, he think I don't know who he is but I know exactly who he is.

"What you gone do?" Mario asked all hyped up.

He was always quick to jump in some shit that had nothing to do with him but that's why he's my perfect fall guy.

A few months back I got caught selling to an undercover agent. The thing about that is, it wasn't much so I kind of agreed to help them catch somebody bigger. The only problem with that is, the people they are looking for don't fuck with me; but Mario's cousin, is one of those big dogs. So I've been implementing different plans and shit to set my boy up because I know he will go ahead and tell on his cousin; then we will both be free.

"I'm gone fuck him up." I said with a frown on my face, even though I was just talking shit. I'd already seen Jaquan get down back when he first moved out here; and I'm not a scary nigga but shit, he gone have to catch a bullet if he ever try to fight me.

"I'm gone help you too my nigga straight up; because that was some hot shit he pulled with yo ole lady." Mario exclaimed as he shook his head.

I didn't even respond to him as I thought about Nakia. That bitch seriously had some nerve pulling some hot shit like that. I couldn't believe how bold she was to go out on a date. I don't give a fuck what her relationship is to that nigga right now because me and her were friends first too, so I know how the shit start.

She's the best thing that has ever happened to me, so I can't lose her. I'm not going to lose her. I need to do some shit to get back in her good graces, but I don't know what I did to piss her off enough to go out with another man.

"Take me by Candace's house." I said and Mario nodded his head.

He did that because he likes Candace, but she won't give him the time of day. Hell, I dropped a few hints here and there but she never pick them hoes up, so I guess she ain't trying to fuck with me either.

A few minutes later, we pulled up to Candace's house but I didn't see Nakia's car out front. She doesn't trust anyone with Amberia but Candace, so I know that she's here. I called

Nakia's phone four times before I got out of the car and each time, she sent me to voicemail.

I made my way to the front door and knocked softly. I knew if I would have knocked hard that Candace wouldn't open the door willingly. Her extra mean ass had to be tricked into opening the door.

"Who is it?" she yelled so I stood off to the side so she couldn't see who I was. I knocked softly again and she swung the door open and peeked her head out. "Oh shit!" she said and tried to close the door but I pushed my way inside of her home.

She launched the glass that she had in her hand at me as she backpedaled further into the house. I used my arm to swat it away. I didn't want to hurt anybody, I just wanted to get my daughter so I could get the hell out of dodge. The only way I knew to teach Nakia a lesson about what she had done was to take away her world. I knew Nakia loved Amberia more than anything, so I had to use her to get my baby back. I can't live without her and if I'm going to have to, that nigga won't be able to live with her.

"Get the fuck outta here nigga!" Candace screamed as she stood in front of her kids and my daughter.
"Amberia come with daddy." I said to her after I saw her peek around Candace's body.

Her lip trembled as she backed away slowly. She was afraid of me. I believed in instilling fear in your children so they won't disobey you, but this isn't what I believed in. I didn't want her to be afraid. She's supposed to trust me.

"Leave her alone and just go." Candace said sternly like she could whoop me.

The bitch couldn't stop me from getting my daughter so she might as well go to the back and get her shoes.

"I'm not leaving here without my daughter. She don't need to be with her hoe ass mama!" I snapped with a look of pure disgust on my face. The thought of that nigga putting his hands on Nakia's body disgusted me completely.

"Hoe? You da hoe nigga! All on Instagram with that ugly ass bitch popping bottles and shit! The fuck you thought was gone happen?!" she yelled back like I wasn't shit.

It didn't matter what I did because I was just being a nigga. That bitch ain't mean shit to me so she doesn't fucking matter.

"Oh you talking real big and bad right now. I bet you put her up to the shit!" I snapped as I tried to calm down but I kept envisioning her deep throating him the way I taught her to deepthroat me.

"I did bitch! And wait til she fuck him just like you fucked that bitch!" Candace screamed and I lost it.

I ran straight to her and slammed her on the ground. She screamed as I delivered blow after blow to her stomach. She tried to swing back but my blows were too powerful. I heard the door open but I thought it was Mario and he knew to stay out of my shit.

I felt a pair of arms grab me and it pissed me off more. I turned around and swung but by the time I realized who it was, it was too late to stop the blow. She hit the hardwood floor and slid across it knocked out cold. I ran to her aid and lift her head up.

"My baby!" Nakia screamed from the doorway.

I felt like shit but I couldn't turn back now. She ran towards me swinging until I backhanded her. Amberia was fine, she could sleep it off at the hotel room that I was about to take her too.

"Give me my baby Kareem!" Nakia screamed as she stood back up to her feet.

She breathed heavily like an animal as she looked at me with tears streaming down her face. I was fucking up but I was going to fix this.

"I love you Nakia. You can't leave me." I pleaded but she folded her arms across her chest as she stared at Amberia. I glanced at her and she was still breathing softly. She was fine.

"It's over Kareem." Nakia said as she tore her eyes away from Amberia just long enough to tell me how she felt. Not a single tear shed as she said it and it made me feel like she really meant it this time.

"It ain't never over baby." I said then turned on the balls of my feet and headed out of the door.

She had another thing coming if she thought she was about to leave me to go be with someone else. I am going to be the only man in my daughter's life and your life. Jaquan ass had to go too. I wasn't about to compete with him for my bitch. She's already mine and she ain't going nowhere. They both might as well find them somebody else to play with.

BAM!

Nakia punched me in the back of my head. "You not taking my daughter."

I sat Amberia down on the floor next to the doorway then stood upright because her licks weren't phasing me. I normally don't hit Nakia in her face but this incident caused for an exception. I punched her so hard she stumbled back and tripped over her nephew and landed on top of her sister. Blood poured from her nose but I didn't care. She needed to learn how to keep her hands to herself any damn way. I bent over, grabbed my daughter and left.

Candace

I had to get off this floor and get to my children that were crying hysterically. I looked up and seen my sister Nakia crawling back towards the wall where her purse was located. I'm not really sure where Nakia's head is right now because Amberia is her world. I turned over on my side and tried to get up. "OUCH!!" I hollered out. That shit wasn't as easy as I thought it would be.

"Mommie are you hurt?" my daughter Nikki asked me with tears in her little doe shaped eyes.

Then her twin brother Niam jumped in with his question. "Yeah mama, why did uncle Kareem hit you like that?" He asked just as I pulled myself up to a standing position. He too had tears in his eyes. I looked around but didn't see my oldest son anywhere.

"Where is your brother?" I asked the twins but they both shrugged their shoulders. I looked around and wondered where he'd run off to.
"We don't know mommy, we were trying to protect you."

To hear my babies say that they were trying to protect me broke my heart in two. My head was spinning, my stomach and ribs were hurting something awful, but I had to find my baby.

"Jayceon!" I called out his name in a panicked state. I called him over and over again before he finally answered.

"Yes ma'am." he said as he approached the stairs. He looked shook up but I couldn't tell if he was afraid of me or Kareem at this moment.

"Baby are you alright?" I asked him. I apologized to all my kids for the what they had witnessed before he had a chance to respond to my question.

"Jayceon what were you doing upstairs?" I asked him.

"I went to my room to hide and call my dad." he stated.

My heart damn near stopped as Jayceon mentioned his dad Mason. My body shook with fear. I had to find out exactly what he told him.

"Umm.." I began not really knowing how to beat around the bush even when it comes to my kids I just asked him. "Jayceon, what did you tell your dad when you called him?" I asked in my mommy voice. You know the one when you're pissed off but don't want to frighten the child. "Twins y'all gone upstairs to your rooms. I need to have a private conversation with y'all brother." I told them because I didn't want them to overhear anything that they shouldn't.

"Oooh Jayceon, you bout to get a butt whipping." Niam teased. Of course Nikki couldn't resist following behind her brother with her little sassy ass.

"Yep!!! He showl is. You know not to be telling mama business stupid."

If the circumstances were different, her statement would have been funny but right now it hurt too much to breathe, so I knew I couldn't laugh. She teased him some more before stomping up the steps. All I could do was shake my head because that little girl is a mess. She knows she acts just like me and my sisters. Now that they are gone, I can focus my attention on Jayceon and what made him call Mason; but before I could get a word out, Jayceon started to apologize. "Mama I'm sorry about calling my dad but Casamoney was hitting you and Aunt Nakia and I was scared."

"So what did you tell your dad when you talked to him?" asked him again growing inpatient. Mason had always been ill tempered and I didn't want him to get in any trouble.

"I told him that Casamoney was beating you and auntie Nakia up; and that he punched Amberia and she hit her head." Jayceon said with all honesty.

"And what did your dad say?" I asked him as I held my breath and waited for a response.

"He said he was on his way to air this house out." he answered.

Oh my God why did I let Mason buy him that damn cell phone. I know y'all don't understand but Mason was an old school player that didn't play no games.

"Okay Jayceon go upstairs and look after your sister and brother please. I have something to take care of down here." I told him then watched him run up the steps.

First things first, I had to check on Nakia because she was no longer in my eye sight; and knowing my sister the way I do, she was probably somewhere calling in the Cavalry on Casamoney's punk ass. One thing about me and my two sisters is that we all had a thing for bad boys and hustlers. We have two brothers that were about that life. After our dad passed, they stepped up to become some of the most ruthless men in these streets.

My body was wrecked with pain as I stumbled thru the house calling my sister's name. I knew she had not left because I would have heard the alarm chime. I heard my phone ringing on the couch as I passed thru the living room. I was headed to the patio because that was the only other place I hadn't checked yet. It was my home girl Brittany's ringtone so I ignored it and opened the patio door. When I opened the door, my sister turned around and her face was drenched in tears and blood. She was pacing back and forth and talking a mile a minute on her cell phone. I don't know who she was talking too but I heard her give my address and tell the person to meet her here.

I went back in the house to get my cellphone and came back out. Nakia had an expression on her face that I had never seen before. My heart broke. I grabbed her in my arms and gave her the biggest hug I could without hurting my ribs and told her that everything would be alright.

"We are going to get Amberia back!" I assured her right before the doorbell rang.

Nakia

I still can't believe the chain of events that has happened today. All I wanted to do was have a good time and get my mind off of Casamoney's trifling ass; and just like clockwork he showed up and ruined my date. But him taking my daughter away from me was not an option. He had definitely crossed the line and I was going to make sure that he felt every bit of pain that he cost me and my sister.

Don't get me wrong, Casamoney was a good father to Amberia. I don't think he would intentionally hurt her, but he would yell at her a lot till the point that she became afraid of him sometimes. I had a problem with that so I would never leave her alone with him for long periods of time.

When I heard my sister's doorbell ring, I became excited and nervous at the same time. Mostly because I knew shit was about to get real. I had put in a few phone calls to some people I knew would ride for the cause; but when she opened the door I had to do a double take because my eyes didn't believe what they were seeing. True enough it was Mason. *'What in the hell is he doing here?'* I thought to myself. I never had a problem with Mason personally. I was just shocked when he started messing with Candace and got her pregnant because of the age difference and the fact that he hung with our pops gambling on the weekends.

"Hey Ladies. Jayceon told me there was a problem over here and that y'all needed some help. So here I am. What's going on?" he asked while carefully examining my sister for marks and bruises.

She was holding her side, so I went to assist her in sitting down. He followed right behind us to the living room.

"Lift your shirt Sis so I can see what's going on." I said to her. She slowly moved her arm from her side and lifted up her tank top. I had to cover my mouth to keep from screaming. "Oh my God! This looks bad Candace you have to go to the hospital." I said.

"I am not going anywhere until we get my niece back home safely." she scolded at me.

We all were high strung so I understand her loyalty, but she was hurt badly and needed to be evaluated by a real doctor. Sure I went to nursing school for a couple of years, but I wasn't qualified to deal with her injuries because they were internal.

"Well at least call your boyfriend and have him come over." I pleaded with her.

Mason didn't even blink when I said that. It let me know that he hasn't changed a bit. He loved Candace and only wanted to see her happy even if that meant not being with him.

Just as she picked up the phone to call Sly, there was another knock at the door. This time I answered the door and it was exactly who I expected; my two brothers Pokey and Dread. I could tell they were already hype and ready to start some shit. They hugged me and told me not to worry because Amberia would be home with me soon.

"That's for damn sure." I heard from behind them.

My brother Pokey let go of me and I opened my eyes to see that it was my boo Jaquan and he wasn't alone. Just like the old days, he never let me down.

"Now that everyone is here, let's get down to business." I said to the group.

"Wait. Before you start anything, what the fuck is Mason's old ass doing here?" Dread asked with venom in his voice.

"Calm down bruh. Regardless of how you feel about Mason he is family and he is here to help. I didn't know he was coming either but since he's here, he can be a great asset to us. Hell, he has connections to people we have only heard of." I said in defense of Mason.

"So right now all personal shit aside, this is for Amberia; and Mason if you are here for any other reason then you can leave. No one in this room will endanger my child's life because you can't work together." I continued.

"With that being said we need to hit these streets and find Casamoney and my daughter. If not them Mario, because he knows everything. Pokey you and Dread hit the east side while me and Jaquan will hit the west side."

"Candace, you stay here with Mason until Sly comes then call me. Mason I know you strapped so you protect my sister and her kids until we get back please. Let's go fellas, we have work to do" I finished and we walked out the door.

When Nakia called me I didn't even let her get a word out because she was crying. All I needed to know was what was the address and I would figure out what was wrong when I got there. I was beyond pissed when I found out Kareem's punk ass had left Olive Garden, went straight to her sister's house and beat both of their asses then took her daughter. That shit was beyond foul and it had me heated enough to revert back to my old ways; that's why I had my boy Melt with me. He and I go way back. His real name is Jamie but we started calling him Melt once we found out that he uses a steel melting machine to melt down the people he used to kill so he wouldn't go to jail. I figure if we're going to kill kareem, we will need Melt's expertise in getting rid of the body.

Nakia followed me to the car and stopped in her tracks once she noticed Melt sitting in the passenger's seat.

"Um… Quan." she called out.

I stopped then turned around to see a hesitant look on her face. We didn't have time for idle chit chat because we needed to find her daughter. I'd turned off my professional self and was now the ruthless street nigga that I'd buried long ago.

"Yeah." I answered slightly agitated.

I was ready to get on the move. Hell I wanted to fuck his punk ass up at Olive Garden but I couldn't because of the witnesses. Not to mention, I'm a corporate man now and can't be doing shit like that publicly.

"Why is Jamie here?" she asked and I cocked my head to the side.

She knew exactly why Melt was here, so there was no need for her to ask me that question. I took a step back and examined her body language. I'd taken many classes to help me read it and I could tell she was beginning to have doubts.

"You know why. What's up?" I asked through squinted eyes.

Her eyes never left Melt as she stood before me. Several seconds passed and her brother Pokey and Dread walked out of the house. Them boys been my niggas since we were tossing pop rocks and soda in our mouths at the same time for the small candy to explode in our mouths.

"What's going on?" Pokey asked after he noticed the way that I looked at his sister. They had always been overprotective so I expected nothing less of them now. I actually expected things to get worse now that they were older.

"Ask ya sister man." I said then walked over to lean against my car.

Melt never acknowledged the fact that we were outside of the car talking about him although he knew exactly what was going on. I guess you could say that he was used to it since he was only called upon for this reason.

Dread had a deep frown etched on his face as he grabbed Nakia by the arm roughly and turned her around. Pokey got pissed off because of how rough Dread was being and I'm not going to lie, I did too but I know this is a family situation.

"Man what the fuck wrong with you?!" Pokey snapped as he pushed Dread so hard that he took several steps backwards. I sighed heavily because we definitely didn't have time for this shit, but I expected nothing else from these two.

When we were growing up, Pokey and Dread use to fight each other all of the time like they were just some random niggas in the streets but would beat the brakes off a mufucker together too, so you couldn't really say anything to them. They're definitely a family that sticks together.

"Man Nakia getting soft and shit!" Dread snapped as he ran up on Pokey and pushed him back.

Pokey countered with a swift blow to Dread's gut that doubled him over which put him in the perfect place to receive an uppercut that sent him flying on his ass.

"Don't put your hands on my damn sister nigga!" Pokey snapped then turned around and walked back over to Nakia. "You getting soft sis?" Pokey asked in a nurturing tone like he hadn't just two pieced their brother.

"No." she began as she shook her head. "I want him dealt with, not dead." she continued and I shook my head.

This nigga had done came in her sister's house and hit both of them, including her daughter, and she didn't want him dead. I didn't understand it at all.

My cell phone started to ring in my pocket and when I saw the name that flashed across my screen, I was tempted to slide it right back in my pocket; but curiosity got the best of me. I walked away from the conversation that they were having to answer the call.

"Yeah?" I answered just before it went to voicemail.

"How are you?" she asked and my body got even more riddled with anger. She'd come along and lead me on for all those years then dipped out without a second notice and wants to know how I am.

"What you want?" I asked as I glanced back. Nakia stared directly at me and for some reason, I felt guilty. It felt like I was in the wrong for answering my own damn phone when me and Nakia aren't even together.

"I miss you." she cooed into the receiver seductively.

My dick jumped but now is not the time to entertain her at all. Hell, really it should never be a time in the future for me to entertain her.

"What you want Miko?" I asked as I mocked an attitude.

"I want some dick baby; and I know you miss how this pussy grip that dick." Miko breathed heavily into the phone.

I had to stop and adjust my dick in my pants before anyone noticed that it was getting hard as I thought about how warm, tight and wet she would always get for me.

"Now is not the time." I said then hung the phone up before she could respond. I closed my eyes and thought about the situation at hand in order to get my dick soft enough to turn around.

"You ready?" I asked Nakia as she shot daggers at me with her eyes.

I didn't know if she'd heard my conversation or if she knew who I was talking to, but it felt like she did. I told myself that nothing was wrong with me answering her call because I was single. Hell, Nakia is the one in a relationship.

"Are you?" she asked with an attitude.

I nodded my head, walked around to the driver's side of my car and hopped in. Nakia climbed in the backseat with so much attitude that it filled the car with so much tension you'd need a machete to cut it.

"Hey Nakia." Melt said.

"Bye Jamie." she responded with her arms crossed over her chest.

"Where do you think he will take her?" I asked and she gave me a shoulder shrug.

She had far too much attitude; and I don't know what kind of fuck shit Kareem let her get away with, but she's not going to be able to keep this funky attitude with me.

"I suggest you lose the fucking attitude or get the fuck out my car." I said to her as I looked directly in her eyes.

Her mouth fell open and I could tell she couldn't believe that I had spoken to her like that, but she had never encountered this side of me.
"I'm good." she said after a couple of seconds passed.

"Are you?" I asked and she nodded her head.

"Try Mario's house." she stated then gave me directions to it.

Miko

I couldn't believe Jaquan hung up on me. I know he's still a bit salty about the way Christian announced our engagement but shit I wanted Jaquan! I had been playing Christian. I didn't really want to be with him. I love Jaquan and I always have; he'd just been so busy at the law firm that he forgot about me. Christian always made time for me. It didn't matter what he had going on, and I loved that about him. The only thing that Christian was lacking was killer sex game. It wasn't bad, but it was below basic. It felt good, but I never came. Hell, I never had one building up.

"Hello?" I answered my ringing phone as I decided to head back to Christian's house since Jaquan is obviously on the bullshit.

"How's my little girl?" My mom cooed into the phone. She's the one that pushed me into making the decision that I made in pretending to want to be with Christian.

"I'm fine mom. How are you?" I asked as I rolled my eyes and shook my head.

"Oh don't roll your eyes at me wench! You not too big for me to put my hands on you!" She threatened.

"But I didn't ma!" I lied as I glanced around. Sometimes I swear it was like she could see me at all times. It was kind of spooky.

"Lie again lil helfa and watch I beat you like a road lizard!" She continued to fuss.

"Yes ma'am." I sighed heavily.

Sometimes it was best to just give in because she was dead serious and would indeed beat me. I didn't know what beating me had to do with a road lizard, but she'd been saying that for years.

"Where's my son in law?" She asked and I could tell by her tone that she was smiling. She found the situation that she'd gotten me in quite comical.

"He's being a butt! I just called him and he hung the phone up on me. I don't know what to do ma." I whined into the phone. I'd just pulled up to Christian's house.

"Now that doesn't sound like Christian at all." She replied sounding worried. She was right, Christian would never hang up on me or brush me off the way Jaquan always has done.

"That's because it wasn't." I responded then held my breath.

"Oh no you don't! You leave that wanna be lawyer alone na. Ya hear me?! Don't go ruining a for sure thing for something that may never be. That's foolishness." She said then groaned out her frustrations.

"I raised you better than this Miko. You have a man that worships the ground you walk on and can take care of you forever! He loves you and wants to marry you girl! Do you know how many women want that?" She continued her rant then waited for me to answer her question.

"I understand ma, but I'm not happy. I love Ja-"

Knock knock knock!!

I dropped the phone in my lap and clenched my shirt around my chest as I stared up at Christian. I painted heavily as I tried to steady my breathing. I lowered the window and glared at him.

"Fuck Christian you scared me!" I snapped at him.

"I'm sorry; but watch your language. Who are you out here talking to?" He questioned suspiciously. That was another thing I hated about him. He was so insecure and always thought I was doing dirt.

I picked my phone back up and placed it to my ear. "Ma, you still there?" I asked and watched as Christian's shoulders relax visibly.

"Yes. Handle your business and call me later baby. I love you." She responded.

"Okay ma, love you too." I said then disconnected the call.

I pulled my keys out of the ignition and climbed out of the car. I glared up at Christian and shook my head. There was no way that I'd be able to spend the rest of my life with him.

"Miko." He called out to my back as I walked past him and headed inside of his house. I was beyond frustrated and I needed to nut.

'I fucking hate Jaquan.' I thought to myself. I knew he'd reconnected with that bitch Nakia with her ugly ass because I saw her run out after him like a lost puppy the night Christian announced our engagement. I'm not a stalker but I followed him the next day and saw that they met for lunch too. So I texted my boy Casamoney and put a bug in his ear. I knew he'd show up and shut shit down.

I met Casamoney a few years back at a block party and he was all over me. I only fucked with him because he was with Nakia and that bitch has always thought she was better than everybody else. I had to show her we were on the same level, so I fucked with Casamoney as heavily as I could; being as though I was still with Jaquan and had just started spending time with Christian. Casamoney is definitely not as talented in the bedroom as Jaquan but I always came, so yeah Christian was definitely rock fucking bottom. I rolled my eyes at the thought just as he stepped behind me and slid his hands down between my legs. Christian definitely had the best foreplay but he could never finish hard for the win. I closed my eyes and laid my head against his chest as he slipped his hand in my panties.

I panted heavily as he massaged my clit. I moaned out as I rotated my hips against his fingers. It felt so good and I could feel my nut rising. I circled my hips faster as I felt his hard dick pressed firmly against my ass.

"Fuck this." He said and removed his fingers. He grabbed me and tried to lead me to the bed but I was so pissed because I was almost there!
"What the fuck Christian?! I was about to cum!" I snapped at him as he ushered me to the bed.

I would have felt better if he would have just bent me over the dresser. I mean how hard is it to be just a little spontaneous? I didn't want to spend the rest of my life fucking only in the bed.

"I got you baby." He said as he pushed me back gently and removed my panties.

He opened my legs and dove in head first. He licked my pussy like a fucking ice cream cone and I just laid there and stared at him. He needed to grow the fuck up because no grown man should be eating pussy like that.

"Mmmh you taste so good." He paused to say then dove back in. I shook my head and just looked at him. "Let me know when you're about to cum." He said and I rolled my eyes. He had the worse head in the world, but you couldn't tell him that.

About five minutes later he stopped and climbed on top of me. I gasped as he entered me slowly. He went in and out of me slowly. I moaned softly as he placed his face in the crook of my neck.

"Ah baby it's so wet." He moaned as he continued to moan. "Ah baby I'm fina cum." He panted as he picked up his pace.

Six quick pumps later he exploded inside of me then rolled over on his side. He draped one arm over my stomach.

"How was it for you?" He asked.

I removed his arm and climbed out of bed. I didn't have to answer that question because he knew it wasn't shit for me.

"Where you going?" He asked but I ignored that question too. I made my way to the bathroom so I could take a shower. Once I finished showering, I walked back into Christian's room to let him know that I was leaving, but he was sleep.

"This can't be life." I said as I turned on the heels of my feet and left out of the house. I really needed to invest in a toy or something.

When I made it to my car I decided to give my boy a call.

"Hello?" He answered with a voice that was filled with panic.

"What's up baby money?" I joked because his ass wasn't balling like he tried to make it seem.

"I fucked up man." Casamoney replied.

"Where are you?" I asked and waited patiently for his answer. The best way to feel better about your problems is to listen to someone else's.

"Best Western. 202." He answered and hung the phone up.

It was good he hung up because I got a real good laugh out of him being at Best Western. Not Casamoney.

I laughed and made my way to the hotel to see what was going on. Hopefully he ain't too distraught that he can't give me some of that fire head that'll have me crawling up the walls.

Nakia

"Lawd help me!" I shouted as I threw my hands in the air. "Why is everybody trying me today?" I continued but only in my head.

I know Jaquan done lost his mind damn mind talking to me like that though. Although I love that thug take control type of nigga in the bedroom. Uh, Uh; this was not the time for it. I had to find my daughter and didn't have time to argue with him; but you can best believe I was going to check his ass just as soon as we were alone. That's the only reason why I pretended like I was good. I had to act like what he said to me didn't make me want to slap his extra sexy ass; but just as soon as Melt wasn't with us, I was going to let him have it.

I know Jaquan very well and this attitude that he has right now is the same one he had growing up. He was a protector back then and to this day nothing has changed. I continued to call Casamoney back to back with no response.

"Dammit!!!" I screamed out of frustration as I got his voicemail once again.

"What's wrong?" Jaquan asked with deep concern etched on his face. I knew I was scaring him but shit, Casamoney was scaring me.
"He won't pick up the phone and I know Amberia is probably terrified of him. I don't know if he took her to the hospital after she was

knocked out. I don't know anything and I feel like this is all my fault. I should have been home with my baby instead of being out on a lunch date with you." I blurted out.

I finally let go of the tears and fear that I had been holding inside. My soul opened up as I thought about all of the times Casamoney had cheated on me, hit me, disrespected me and our daughter. His disrespectful ass even had a bitch staying at my house and driving my car while I was out of town at my grandfather's funeral. It was all too much to handle as I cried my heart out.

Jaquan pulled in the parking lot of the Quik Trip and tried to console me. I was embarrassed as hell for showing such weakness in front of my peers, but I have heard older people say pressure bust pipes. I guess it's true because my heart was bursting at the seams. Jaquan put his arms around me then pulled me close to him. He stroked my hair and whispered in my ear.

"Sssh....it's going to be alright." he repeated more than once. "We are going to find this punk ass nigga and get your baby back; I promise Nakia." he assured me.

I really had my doubts since we had been riding around for hours with no sign of either of them but for some reason I believed Jaquan's promise. He had never let me down before.

"Walk thru" By Rich Homie Quan began blaring from the back seat breaking up our intimate moment. It was Melt's phone ringing. Up until that moment it had slipped my mind that his crazy ass was still in the car. I know I call a lot of people crazy, but Melt is really throwed off. I mean he my boy and all but he be on some ole Hannibal Lecter type of shit. I mean if you have to kill a nigga, kill em; but all that mutilation and stuff is nonsense. Wait, on second thought maybe he was on to something. *'He could be just the person I need to teach Kareem a lesson.'* I thought to myself. I would never kill Kareem but I am going to make sure that the next time he see me he put some respect on my name. It's going to be something he will never forget. Ump....just thinking about it caused a devious smile to spread across my face.

"Aye Bruh, I need you to swing me back by the spot I got some business to attend to." Melt said a little too happy for my taste.

When we pulled up to Melt's house, I was expecting it to be some rundown shack or a slaughter house even; considering what he does and the fact that I knew nothing of him having a real job. It was a nice two story home with a two-car garage. To say that I was shocked would be an understatement.

"Aye call me if yall hear anything." Melt said as he got out of the car.

We agreed and pulled off into the night. I was exhausted but I told Jaquan to hit the blocks once more before calling it a night. I decided to try calling Casamoney's phone one last time. Ring... Ring... After the third ring I began to lose hope again.

"Hello?" he answered in his childlike demeanor. It was the reason I fell in love with him in the first place.

"Kareem! Where is my daughter?" I asked him as I tried to stay as calm as possible.

He burst out laughing as if I had told a joke or something. It pissed me off! I put my finger up to my lips in a sssh motion then hit the speaker button on my phone and turned the radio down. I was trying to see if I could hear any background noises that would tell me where he was.

"Why you questioning me like that baby ma? Ain't she my daughter too? Or is she?" he asked as he continued to laugh. "But to answer your question, Amberia is right here playing." he said.

"Where are you? Please let me come get my daughter or you bring her home!" I pleaded with him. "We can forget all about this, I just want my baby back. I promise I won't call nobody or tell the police if that's what you worried about." I continued.

Silence.

"Amberia is all I have in this world and she's your daughter!" I screamed at him accidentally. This whole situation had me acting out of character. "Let me come get her. I'm sure she's scared and confused."

"No. You don't deserve to have my daughter you are a slut." He whispered into the phone. "That punk ass nigga will never play daddy to my seed or have my woman; so both of you better watch your back because I'm coming." he paused. "If I can't have you no one will. Make up your mind." he spat then hung up in my face.

"NO! NO! NO!" I screamed as I punched the car's window over and over. "I swear on everything I love I'm going to kill him if he hurt my daughter in any way. Maybe I'll just kill him anyway." I said calmly.

Candace

When I heard the keys in the door I knew it was Sly. He's my baby daddy and fiance. I knew he was coming since Nakia insisted that I call him and tell him what had happened.

"Baby?" he called out as he came in the house. I was in the den on the sofa but I was too sore to move.

"In here." I called out weakly from where I was laying.

"Babe what the hell happened?" he asked in a state of confusion.

"Ouch!" I screamed as I tried to sit up straight. I told him every detail from beginning to end and could see the shocked look on his face. His bottom jaw dropped in awe.

"So you trying to tell me that Casamoney bust into this house, beat up you, Nakia and Amberia too basically then kidnapped her?" Sly asked with a confused look on his face

"Yes Sly, that's exactly what I'm saying!" I said a little too loud. My stomach muscles ached a bit so I eased back down on the couch.

"Where were the rest of the kids when this was happening?" he asked with fire in his eyes.

"Ohh.....hell, I knew this was coming." I said as I rolled my eyes into the back of my head. Don't get me wrong I totally understood his anger, but I didn't feel like being the one getting the backlash of some shit I didn't do. I had no control over that.

"I'm sorry I didn't hear you." he said as he leaned his ear closer in my direction.

I hate when his ass is being sarcastic, because he knows damn well where the kids were. The same place they ass always at, which is right under me. I stared at him in silence with my lip poked out as I prayed that he would let it go, but I had no such luck.

"Umm.. Candace I'm not playing with you girl. I want to know where my kids were when Casamoney put his hands on you and their auntie." he snapped again.

Trying to keep this charade up was useless because either way they were going to beat his ass.

"Okay Sly, the kids were watching from the steps. Everything just happened so fast I didn't have time to get them to their rooms first." I said as I grunted loudly due to the pain as I tried to stand up.

Sly attempted to help me but only made me scream louder. It must have been louder than I thought because this time Mason ran down the stairs.

"Candace are you okay?" he asked genuinely concerned.

"Yeah, she alright old man." Sly stated. Mason continued to walk towards me to see for himself.

Neither one of my baby daddies were lightweights with their hands. I had seen both of them in action on several occasions. I was just glad that they never came to blows. It was no secret that they didn't care for each other. The only thing that keeps my mind at ease in this situation is the fact that they both loved and respected me and my kids. Sly took care of Jayceon just like he did the twins. Mason was no different; when Sly was fucking up in these streets going in and out of jail and messing with these hoes, he took care of everyone just the same. Shid, the way I look at it, we all family and needed to act accordingly.

Mason helped me walk to the front door by putting his arm around my back and thru my arm so most of my body weight was on him. Sly was getting an attitude.

"Man get your damn hands off her!" he hollered at Mason.

"Lift up her shirt." Mason demanded.

"What? I'm not lifting her shirt in front of you my dude." Sly snapped back angrily.

"I swear you young niggas is as dumb as they come." Mason remarked. "I have a child with this woman do you honestly think that I don't know what every part of her body look like fool? I was trying to show you her ribs because she needs to go to a hospital, she is bleeding internally." Mason paused. "Now lift her damn shirt!" Mason hollered this time scaring even me.

'Oh it hurts so bad.' is all that was going thru my head as Sly lifted up the tank top I was wearing. It must have looked pretty bad because in the next breath he was telling the kids to come get in the car. Mason ended up carrying me to Sly's car and buckling me in.

"Get her to the hospital, I'll check with yall later to see how she's doing. I have some work to do." he told Sly. He kissed my son on the head and jumped in his car.

All the way to the hospital Sly ranted and raved about how he was going to find Kareem and punish his ass for disrespecting his home and putting his hands on me. Tears began to roll down my cheeks as he sped into the emergency room parking lot at Emory University. Don't get it twisted, I wasn't no weak bitch. I've had my share of fights and had even been stabbed before, but none of it equaled to this pain. Maybe it was because I never fought a man before.

I must have passed out or something because when I woke up, machines were beeping, my ribs were bandaged, and I had an

69

I.V. in my arm. I panicked and tried to get up but was stopped by a sharp pain in my chest. I heard a voice say, "Babe calm down." then Sly appeared from the corner of the room. From the look of his eyes, he had been sleeping. He walked over and kissed my lips with so much passion that it felt like I was in heat. When it was over, he told me how scared he was that I was going to die. He also told me that I had lost a lot of blood and they had to operate on me twice in twenty four hours. While Sly explained everything that had happened all I could think about was the reason all this shit got started in the first place. Yes, I will admit my part in this chaos because I shouldn't have ever showed Nakia the picture of Casamoney with some random hoe in the club. But I was just tired of men getting away with everything while the woman had to buckle down and be responsible. Some women at least but I knew that Casamoney was the father of our sister Angela's baby too and he knew I knew. So when Nakia told me about running into Jaquan, I couldn't resist trying to bring her some happiness. She deserved someone who would treat her right.

Mason

I have only loved two women in my whole forty-six years of life, my wife and Candace. My wife had passed years before Candace even came along though. I knew messing with her at such a young age was wrong being that I was damn near fifteen years older, but my mama told me when I was just a little boy that your heart wants what it wants; and in my case it was Candace Willis.

I met her and her siblings when I use to gamble with their pops. Yes lawd, me and Melvin had some good times back then. He went into the army, served his country and came home. Two years later he was robbed and killed in front of the same street corner I run today. Nothing happens in this city without me knowing it but today, this shit was a shock.

As I sat in my car and watched the neighborhood kids run around laughing and playing, it made me sad. It also made me wonder about my own son. I wondered what kind of man he is going to be when he grows up. What kind of sports will he play and if Sly will love and protect him like I do? Jayceon is the splitting image of me when I was younger. I have two other children that I really messed up with. I have a grown son in prison for murder and a grown daughter that ran off and married the white boy lawyer who prosecuted her brother. I haven't spoken to Felica in over ten years. When I found out Candace was having

Jayceon I was ecstatic. I finally had a chance to do it right.

I know that Pokey and Dread hated my guts for sleeping with their little sister and so did their mom, but me and Candace had a special love that could not be broken. Our relationship became strained once she found out I was pimping; but no matter how much I tried to convince her that I would never cross that line with her or treat her with any type of disrespect, she couldn't handle it and decided to break it off. I was hurt but I couldn't be mad because I understood where she was coming from. She was raised with morals and didn't want her son growing up around that environment. Most of them were like that, but I'm not sure what went wrong with her sister Angela. She was one of my best hoes up until a few years ago when she fell in love with her first baby daddy. Notice I said first baby daddy because word on the street is that baby four and five belong to her sister Nakia's boyfriend Kareem. From what I can see, they telling the truth. Ray Charles can see that that's that boy baby.

I think the reason that Nakia is probably the only one in the state that don't know Casamoney is the father of her nephew is because her mind won't allow it. I know for a fact that the thought has crossed her mind on more than one occasion. For God sakes, they even got the same identical baby blue eyes as Casamoney and Amberia; but in her mind, that's even too low for him to stoop and no one wants to believe that their sister would do that so she ignore it.

"Damn I just don't know if a relationship can come back after something like that." I said as I shook my head.

That is why I'm trying so hard to fix my mistakes with Candace and her family. I don't want no ill feelings and drama between us which is the reason I have kept this secret so long. No, not about the liver cancer, but the other one.

Jaquan

Nakia and I rode around town for hours trying to find this nigga and Amberia. I still couldn't believe he'd gone and not only taken his daughter but knocked her out too. That was some cold-blooded shit rather he tried to or not. That man didn't give a damn about nobody but himself and he couldn't stand the sight of seeing Nakia with another man. That's why his simple-minded ass decided to go and take his own child. He knew that was the only way Nakia would go back to him. I've always thought it was crazy, the measures niggas would go through to get a chick to come back, but won't do what they need to do to ensure that they won't leave.

Given the sentencing that he's facing, he's going to need someone as solid as Nakia on his side to ride the bid off with him if my boss can't get him off with no jail time served and I think he knows it. That's probably why he went through such drastic measures to get her attention. At the same time though, Nakia is a good girl; so that was probably her first time doing something like that, so she got his attention too.

She'd called him several times and he made it clear what he wanted, her. I had no doubt in my mind that she would go back though. Even if it was only for Amberia, but I guess I couldn't blame her. Every woman wants a family, but hopefully she sees that she will never be happy with him. Then it's going to be awkward with him coming around anyway because he beat her sister Candace up pretty bad from the looks of things.

My phone started to vibrate in my lap and when I looked down and saw that it was Miko calling again, I hurry up and hit decline. I had nothing for the triflin bitch, not even dick. Ever since I found out about her and Christian's engagement, it seems like she's been trying harder and harder to get me to come around and give her another chance. She'd sent me thousands of text messages apologizing, but it was just too late to apologize. I was over the bullshit.

Women could deal with more shit than men could and I'd reached my limit quick with Miko. Rather the engagement was real or not, she'd been dealing with both of us and that's some shit I can't come back from. I'd never trust her so being with her would be pointless.

The person I really wanted to talk to was Christian though. No words had to be spoken because I wanted to let my hands do the talking. He'd gone against the grain and started messing with my girl, my woman. It didn't matter that he knew I didn't love her, to him she was off limits and he violated.

"What are you thinking about?" Nakia asked as she stared down at her phone. I looked over at her and her hand trembled slightly, so I knew she was only trying to distract herself from her current situation.

"The truth?" I asked because I didn't know if she was ready for me to be open and honest about how I felt about everything. Not anything about her situation, but everything about mine. Nakia has always had a way of listening selectively. She'd hear everything you said but would only respond to what she thought was important.

She placed her phone down then rotated her body to the side and looked at me. I could tell that she was attempting to read my body language, but I'd become a pro at masking all of my emotions. Pretending to love someone wasn't easy, but I'd done it with Miko for a while now thinking I'd grow to love her eventually.

"Always." she said once she realized she wasn't going to be able to get anything solely off of how I drove my car through the streets.

I allowed my eyes to roam the cars that sat idly on the side of the road as the patrons walked into different establishments. I tried to get my thoughts together instead of just talking but it proved harder than I expected. I silently hoped that she'd grown a bit and tried to understand where I was coming from rather than flipping things around.

"I was thinking about Miko and Christian." I answered honestly.

Tension filled the car immediately. I glanced over at her as she sat stiff as a board and stared at me. I knew the mere mention of Miko's name would do something to her, but I didn't expect it to alter her mood this much. You would think I was fucking them both at the same time or something the way she looked at me.

"Why?" she asked as she tried to play it cool but she shook her right foot slightly and that had always been a telltale sign of her anger rising. It was a like a warning to choose your next words wisely or shit could and more than likely would hit the fan.

"She keeps calling me. I was just thinking about the betrayal from them both." I answered and her shoulders relaxed, so I knew she had done calmed down. I didn't understand why hearing someone's name could alter her mood but I didn't want to get into that. We had more pressing matters at hand, plus Miko was calling my phone again.

"Why won't you answer?" she asked and it kind of bothered me because I knew why she was asking.

Women only want to discuss your ex when they want you to tell them something bad that will reassure them that they're better. I gave her a shoulder shrug instead of answering her question.

"Don't ignore her on my account." Nakia said with a shrug then turned around to face the front.

I knew she just wanted to pick a fight at this point because she was in her feelings about her baby daddy, but she didn't need to take shit out on me and I wasn't about to go back and forth with her about nothing. She sucked her teeth when I didn't respond.

"You know what Quan? I don't know why you were with her anyway." she said then rolled her eyes and I couldn't believe my ears.

I thought about what she'd said and in all honesty, I didn't know why I was with her either but that didn't give her the right to say that or even feel that for that matter.

"Yeah; and I don't know why you been with Kareem's ole good for nothing, community dick having ass! Sweep around your own front door Nakia. I'm sure that nigga been dogging you out since y'all been dating. Know your worth ma." I said and felt bad as soon as the words left my mouth.

She was already going through a lot and the last thing I wanted to do was bring her more pain, but I'd done just that. I glanced at her just as she sucked her bottom lip in. I knew she was trying to keep it from trembling because I'd struck a nerve. She probably didn't know if she wanted to cry, hit me or both.

"I'm sorry Nakia." I said as I reached over to grab her hand but she snatched it away from me and folded her arms across her chest. When she turned her head to look out of the passenger's seat window, I knew she'd allowed the tears to drop and just didn't want me to see them.

Her phone started ringing in her lap. She glanced down then looked at me with a confused tear stained face then answered the call.

"Hello?" she answered the phone. I turned the radio completely off so she could hear whoever it was calling her clearly. I hoped it was Kareem telling her where to come pick Amberia up from because I needed to get home and work on my cases.

"What? Is she okay?" she asked and her leg began to shake so hard it rocked the car a bit. "It's not my fault Sly!" she continued then a deep frown graced her face. "I'm on my way." she replied calmly. I couldn't hear what Sly was saying to her but whatever it was, was clearly pissing her off.

"Fuck you! That's my sister! I'm on my way!" she snapped then hung the phone up. "Candace is in the emergency room." she stated and I drove straight there.

Before I could say anything to her, she hopped out of the car and made her way inside. I don't think I have to tell you she slammed my door and didn't say bye or anything.

I shook my head as I drove off. My nerves were on edge because I was hoping Nakia and I could rekindle an old flame but we both had entirely too much going on right now.

She wasn't established with anything of her own yet and neither was I. She already had a daughter and baby daddy problems, but I didn't; although I knew Miko would become a problem.

Miko

I could believe Cassamoney's ass had me bent over the toilet in the hotel room while his daughter watched TV in the room. Normally I wouldn't do anything that extreme, but my hatred for her fuck ass mama made it all worthwhile. I swear I never liked Nakia's good girl ass; and that's why I pursued Jaquan in the first place.

Now her sister Angela, that was my roll dog and she'd told me about the crush Nakia had on Jaquan, so I swooped in and snatched him up before she could; and now she thinks she's about to come and snatch him back. Yeah, over my dead body. Jaquan is the best man I ever had and I'm not letting go and I'm not marrying Christian's lame ass either.

I didn't ask Cassamoney anything about why he had his daughter at a room when he lived with her or nothing, because it wasn't my business. All I wanted was some good meat and once I got it, I left. But sex ain't better than love and I know I don't act like it, but I love Jaquan. My only problem with him was his lack of time. That's how I ended up messing with Christian. He made time for me and made me feel special, so I kind of felt like I was supposed to make him feel better too and what better way than to make him think I was leaving Jaquan for him?

Christian fucked me up though announcing the engagement publicly. I hadn't told anyone about it for the specific reason that I wasn't going to marry him. It was fun as hell to have my cake and eat it toom, but Christian got shit confused if he thinks I would really leave Jaquan to be with him.

Having them both is like the perfect man. Jaquan is so focused on his career that whoever he's with is going to be sacrificed because all of his time and energy going to his career; but he's the best lover I've ever had, and I've had quite a few.

Then there's Christian, the hopeless romantic. He makes time for you, takes you out on dates and he's already established; but his sex is mediocre to say the least. It's okay when nothing else is available, but it's not satisfactory. Plus he's lame! Oh my gosh his jokes are the worse and he's always joking about something stupid.

I've realized my mistake now and I want Jaquan and only Jaquan. I know it's hard to believe when Cassamoney just dicked me down but aye, a woman has needs too; and I just like to get mine satisfied. I'm not for the double standard.

Anyway, I'm willing to be a sacrifice in Jaquan's life as long as I can still be a part of it because I love him and I know he's going to make it; and he fucks me silly when he has time. I just can't get him to answer the phone and it's driving me crazy! I wanted to text him and tell him how I feel but I can't have any evidence getting to Christian in case Jaquan don't take me back. I'm no dummy, so if I have to be with

Christian then I will be and I'll just do my thing on the side to get my pleasure. I'll laugh at all them damn corny ass jokes if I have to.

I headed to my mom's house so I could take a shower and hang out. Christian is in town and I can't go home with Cassamoney's nut sliding down my leg. It felt disgusting as is, but he just doesn't like using condoms. I'm on birth control, so it's fine. I called Jaquan one more time as I pulled in my mom's yard and surprisingly he answered.

"What do you want Miko damn?!" he yelled into the receiver.

I'm not going to lie like it didn't hurt my feelings the way he yelled at me, but I deserved it for hurting him. He could pretend like he didn't care about my engagement to his best friend, but anyone with common sense would know that that will hurt anybody.

"You. Baby I'm so sorry. I fucked up. Please let me make it up to you." I said to him.

Any time we've ever had any type of problem, I'd fuck him real good and nasty like a porn star and all would be forgiven; so I knew if I could just get my hands on him, that everything would be fine.

"I'm good on you Miko. I wish you nothing but the best." he said then hung the phone up in my ear.

I sighed heavily because I hated to do what I was about to do, but he'd left me no choice. Okay, I really didn't hate what I was about to do. I raised one leg and began to circle my fingers around my clit. I was already sloppy wet from fucking with Cassamoney, so it made it a little hard to apply steady pressure. I rotated my hips and moaned softly as I grabbed my phone and called the number I'd memorized from her calling Cassamoney's phone while we were just together.

"Uh, aaah!" I moaned as she answered her phone. "Ooooh just like that Quan baby!" I closed my eyes and imagined Jaquan's warm mouth wrapped around my pussy as he sucked hard on my clit. "Aaah fuck Quan I'm fina cum!" I screamed as my legs began to tremble.

I screamed out in pure ecstasy as I road my orgasm out then glanced at the phone. "Damn I've missed you Jaquan. I love you." I said and Nakia hung her phone up.

I hopped out of my car with a bright smile on my face as I made my way to my mom's door. I used my key to let myself in and tried to sneak past her and head straight to the bathroom, but she caught me before I could.

"We not speaking huh?" my mom asked as she wiped her hands off on her apron.

I sighed and made my way to her. The cum was drying and it felt disgusting and sticky.

I knew I had an uncomfortable look on my face to match how I felt too.

"I'm sorry ma. Hey." I said as I threw one arm around her to hug her.

"Move. Bath now! Trifling helfa." my mom said as she pushed me off of her with a frown on her face. I gave her shoulder shrug then turned around to head to the bathroom. "You lost one good man, don't lose another one for a nut." she yelled at my back but I ignored her because I didn't want to hear any of that.

I hopped in the shower and washed my body thoroughly. It felt so good to be free. If only I was financially free on my own then I wouldn't need to be with someone who would take care of me. I dried my body off, lotioned up and walked to my room because I had an entire wardrobe at my mom's house. I decided on sweatpants and an Aeropostale t-shirt with flip flops so I'd be comfortable. I planned to lounge around my mom's place all day and eat whatever it was that she was whipping up in the kitchen. Once I was clean and comfortable, I headed back to the kitchen.

I grabbed my ringing phone off the counter and saw that it was Christian calling me. I made my way to the living room and took a seat. I needed to get comfortable before I talked to him and that included finding me a good show to watch. Plus I knew he would hang up and call right back until he got me.

"Hello?" I answered as I laid back on the couch and crossed one leg over the other one.

"Why haven't you been answering your phone?" he breathed heavily into his receiver.

I rolled my eyes because he didn't understand how much he irritated me with that. I hated being tracked and that was something else I loved about Jaquan, when he saw he saw me he never blew me up the way Christian does.

"I'm fine how are you?" I asked sarcastically but I knew he knew I had a attitude.

"Don't get cute with me Miko I've been-"

"You know what Christian? I've been giving you all of my time and the day I choose to come spend the day with my mom, you call going off! I'm just going to stay here a couple of days!" I snapped then hung up the phone.

He called me back immediately but he should know by now that I'll be back and I just needed a breather. I really needed more time away from him so I could show Jaquan I was serious.

Christian

I paced back and forth in my living room as I called Miko over and over again. I loved her so much but I didn't trust her. I mean look at how I got her, who would trust her. The only reason I asked her to marry me is to show her I'm the one that's willing to take care of her. Jaquan never loved her and I knew that for a fact. He always told me he didn't love her and he showed her that he didn't. They were together for years and he never made a move to marry her. Hell, I don't think the thought to marry her ever crossed his mind; so you would think she'd be a little more grateful. I wanted to be with her, love her, have kids with her and grow old with her, but now things were changing. We were fine until I announced our engagement publicly. She got mad but I didn't understand why she was mad. I love her and I wanted the world to know including Jaquan.

I haven't seen or talked to him since then and it's by choice. Now I will admit that it was fucked up the way I did it, but the heart wants what the heart wants. I've wanted to tell him about Miko and I for a while, but I didn't know how. I didn't mean to hurt him though. That was my boy. We were like brothers, but I honestly didn't think he would care that I was with her. I mean damn, it had been full nights she'd stay with me and he never called her to see where she was or anything, so I honestly didn't think it mattered. She was living with me for months before I proposed to her and I never saw where he called her. That's why I call her so much. He lost her because he wasn't paying her any attention. He didn't give her enough time, so I was willing to give her my full attention and all of my time; which is why I'd quit playing ball. I quit so I could devote myself to Miko completely and be home around the clock. I'd already applied at Lowe's and got the job, so the money wouldn't stop coming in. I knew the money wouldn't be the same, but I knew she wasn't with me for my money. We had a love like no other.

That's why I was about to go to her mom's house and make sure she was okay. I needed to make sure we were good, but I wasn't ready to tell her the news of me quitting yet. I'm sure she will be happy, but I'm waiting until we tie the knot. It will be much better once we start having kids if I'm home to help her with the kids rather than being gone somewhere playing ball missing important parts of their lives. I slipped my shoes on, grabbed my keys and headed to her mom's place.

Her mom didn't live far from me so it didn't take long for me to get there. My heart filled with joy when I pulled up and saw her car parked in the driveway. I got out and walked over to the car and touched the hood of it. I got mad immediately because she'd told me that she'd been at her mom's house all day but if that was true then the hood of her car wouldn't be warm. I marched straight up to the door and knocked like the police.

"What the fuck?!" Miko yelled as she swung the door open with an attitude.

She squinted her eyes at me as she looked at me like she couldn't believe that I was knocking on the door like the police. Or maybe she couldn't believe I'd actually showed up.

"I'm sorry." I apologized quickly as I took in her attire. She had her hair pulled up into a loose ponytail with sweatpants and no makeup on. I suddenly felt like shit because I knew Miko and she would never go out in public like that.

"For what Christian? Blowing up my phone like maniac or beating on my mama's door like the police? What is your problem?" she asked with a frown her face. I couldn't help but notice she never moved to the side so I could enter. I glanced around her to see if I could see anyone inside that shouldn't be here.

"What are you looking for Christian? I swear you're losing it." she said as she shook her head and attempted to close the door. I blocked it and pushed it all the way open. I couldn't let her shut me out without explaining.

"I was coming to see you and your moms but your hood, the hood was warm and I got mad." I explained honestly but she looked confused.

"The hood?" she asked with a frown on her face. "Wait, the hood of my car? You checked the hood of my car? Did you ever consider the fact that it's hot as hell outside and maybe that's why the hood is warm?" she asked as she gave me the side eye. I felt so stupid and shame.

"I'm sorry." I reiterated because I didn't know what else to say. I loved her and I didn't want to lose her.

"You damn right you are!" she said with her arms folded firmly across her chest as she glared at me. "I don't know what I was thinking being with you. You don't even trust me and if we don't have trust we don't have nothing." she stated too calm for my liking.

"Look how I got you!" I snapped but regretted it as soon as the words left out of my mouth. She looked at me and nodded her head.

"Touche' Christian touche'." she said then went to close the door again, but I wasn't having it. I wasn't about to let her go. I'd invested too much time in her to let her walk away. I'd let my dream go and everything, if I let her go too then I'd end up with nothing.

"Baby listen, I didn't mean-"

"No you did. You just didn't mean for me to find out. It's cool, I understand. I'm done." she said and tried to close door again.

I shoved the door so hard that the glass in the middle of wooden door shattered. Miko's eyes widened with fear as she took a couple of steps backwards.

"I'm sorry Miko but I can't lose you." I told her as she continued to walk backwards.

Her mom rushed around the corner and looked at the door then checked Miko out to make sure that she was okay before she turned back to me.

"You need to leave." her mom said firmly.

I backed away slowly and stared at Miko the entire time. I didn't mean to scare her or break her mom's door and I planned on getting it fixed but one thing for certain and two things for sure, Miko is mine now and I'll be back to get her.

<u>Nakia</u>

When I jumped out of Jaquan's truck and slammed the door I was hotter than a devil's toenail. One because Sly had called my phone to tell me that my sister had been taken into surgery to stop the bleeding she had internally and he thought it was best if I stayed away from her for a while. If he thought for one minute that I would listen to his ass and not come see about my blood, he had lost his mind and probably needed to see a doctor about it quick. When I got there, I ran to the nurse's station and gave her my name.

"Excuse me ma'am, I'm looking for my sister Candace Willis."

She typed her name in the computer system and a few seconds later, she told me that she was still in surgery and that I could wait in family room 3 to the left.

You would think I would know my way around this hospital since I worked upstairs, but it was set up completely different in the emergency room. I could hear voices before I even entered the room. I walked in and immediately laid eyes on Sly's big brother Moe. It was always a pleasure to see his over sexy ass, but I had more pressing matters to worry about right now.

"Hey." he stood up to hug me like the gentleman he was.

"Is there any news on my sister yet?' I asked as I hugged his neck.

"No we still waiting." he replied.

Sly had his back turned to us from the time I walked in the door because he was deeply engaged in a phone conversation. I'm not sure who he was talking too but from the tone in his voice I could tell it wasn't a pleasant conversation. When he ended his phone call, he turned around in our direction.

"I thought I told you not to come down here and to stay aw-" before he could even finished his sentence I mushed his face hard as hell.

"You better get out my face with that bullshit. Nobody tells me what to do when it comes to my sisters!" I snapped with a deep frown etched on my face.

"It's your damn fault that she's in here!" he shouted at me and kicked a nearby chair. Moe stood up to intervene.

"Look, both of you need to calm down we are all here because we are concerned about Candace's well-being so let's just chill out until the doctor come tell us something."

Sly and I were still engaged in a stare down like two deranged bulls. I knew he would stand his ground and that's what I liked about the nigga, but he also knew I wasn't going to back down either. Moe was right though, this was not the time to be at each other's throats, we needed to stick together.

I plopped down in a chair feeling defeated. I closed my eyes and began to pray to God. When I was done, I started to focus and think more clearly. I need to call Angela and tell her what's going on. I really didn't like talking to this chick with her over the top bourgeois ass, but she was our sister and she needed to be here. Plus, I know Candace would have been feeling some type of way if I didn't. She was always so big on how family should stick together. Not me, if you acted like you didn't like me or care for my company, I let you be and kept pushing. That's why I didn't fool with Angela to much because every time we around each other, she be looking at me crazy. If I said anything about my job or something I wanted to do for Amberia, she would roll her eyes or say some sarcastic shit like "you think you and your daughter better than everybody else" with venom in her voice.

The last time was about three months ago standing in our mama's kitchen. I was in there discussing the details of Amberia's tiara and toddler party with my mom and Candace when she stopped by with her four kids. She walked in, grabbed a water out of the refrigerator and sat down next to mom at the table. The only part she really heard was I was trying to keep everything under a thousand dollars before she jumped in and called me a stupid bitch for spending that much money on a child that young. I don't know what came over me but I wasn't in the mood for her shit that day and I snapped off.

"Let me tell you something hoe. I don't know why you always hating on me and my daughter; and I don't think no amount of money is too much for my child, that's why I bust my ass on my job. Maybe if you wasn't dick hopping all the time you would have somebody to help you provide better shit for your kids."

The look on her face was priceless, I knew she was mad when she jumped up from the table and headed in my direction.

"Don't even do it to yourself, because if you get in my face I'm going to beat the living hell out of you." I told her meaning every word.

I guess she thought about it and decided to get her kids and go. That was the best thing she could have ever done. Now it's kind of like fuck being sisters. I know she don't like me and the feeling is mutual. I just needed to wrap my mind around being around her for Candace.

'It'll only be a couple of hours.' I thought to myself as I dialed her number.

Angela

I had just finished feeding the kids and was getting ready to take a shower before work when my phone rung. I got excited because most of the time when my phone ring it's about getting money or some of Casamoney's dick. I giggled to myself while jumping on my bed to grab the phone. My smile was quickly turned upside down when I saw it was my sister Nakia calling. *'What in the hell could this dingy bitch want?'* I thought as I hit the answer key.

"Hello." I said as dry as possible. I didn't want to talk to her because I really didn't like the bitch.

"Angela I need you, can you please come down to Emory hospital? Our sister is here." I looked at the phone as if I could see her because I couldn't believe she was damn near begging me to be there.

"Nakia, slow down and tell me what's going on." I said as I got out of the bed and began to throw some clothes on while she explained everything that had happened from her and Jaquan at the restaurant, to Casamoney jumping on them and knocking Amberia unconscious. My mouth hung open in disbelief.

I could not believe what she was saying and it sounded like a movie or a best-selling book, but I had never known Nakia to lie to none of us. I could tell she was a nervous wreck too, so I believed her.

"Okay Nakia, let me get my neighbor to watch the kids and I'm on my way." I told her as I put my shoes on.

I called my oldest son Demarcus and told him to go next door and ask Shanda, their babysitter to come here.

"Yes ma'am." he said before racing his younger siblings to the door.

I needed a few minutes to try and process what Nakia had just told me. When Shanda walked into my bedroom, I knew she could tell something was wrong by the look on my face but I didn't have time to explain. I just told her I had a family emergency and that I'll pay her extra for coming earlier. She agreed and I left.

I jumped in my new Jeep Liberty and hit the highway but I kept trying to call Casamoney. I had been calling him since early this morning and he hasn't called back yet. That was unusual because he never put me or our son on hold and he calls to check on our soon to be baby. After about three more times I gave up. I started to feel bad for the first time in three years for doing my sister wrong, especially hearing her cry like that over my niece and sister. It kind of pulled at my heartstrings.

I'm always mean to my sisters, well I'm mean to Nakia. She has never done anything to me but I was jealous of her life and I wanted a man like Casamoney that had good looks, a little money and some fye ass dick. I was really trying to find my own baller but then he showed up at my job one night they were fighting and paid for a private dance. Most people would have walked back out of the door when they saw their sister's baby daddy sitting there, but not me. I wanted that money and anything else he was offering.

I smiled because I was a little shy at first, but I'm a stripper and this is what I do. I got my confidence back quickly and put on a mind-blowing show for him. He was throwing them dollars and I was shaking my ass. We both were having a good time, so when the room attendant came around he paid for another hour. We ordered a couple of blue motherfuckers and tequila shots, smoked a blunt of Kush and a few minutes later, things turned physical. He asked me to twerk for him one more time. I stood above him and bounced my ass until he pulled me down on his lap and kissed me. I had been kissed many times before, but when Kareem kissed me that night it was magical. He didn't kiss me like I was a stranger or a trick, he kissed me with passion like I was his woman and I got carried away with the feeling of being loved and wanted.

I could tell that he was high and horny but so was I so I went for it. I removed my little outfit that was barely covering anything anyway, so I could have left it on. I was still positioned on his lap, so I began placing soft kisses on his neck and chest. When he started moaning my name in that deep New Orleans drawl, all my logic went out the window. I started unbuttoning his shirt and fell deeper in lust. His hairs were soft and laid neatly on his chest.

"Oooh...you sexy baby." I moaned as I looked into his blue eyes.

I wanted to see more of his body but I realized we only had about twenty minutes left to get it popping. I snatched his shorts down like a woman on a mission and got back on top of him. As I stared down at his dick I couldn't help but think that it was everything that I'd hoped for. It was long and thick with a perfectly round mushroom head. The harder it got, the wetter I got. The anticipation of feeling him pounding away inside of me was killing me slowly. Just as I was a about to cum he lifted me up then bent me over the table in front of us and gave exactly what I was wanting. The shit felt so good that it brought tears to my eyes.

"Ahh! Kareem I'm about to cum baby, please don't stop!" I begged him as he drilled me harder.

"Ugh...me too!" he groaned before pulling out and nutting all over my ass.

I was disappointed because I wanted feel his cum inside of me, but I didn't let the disappointment show. He was looking for something to wipe off with but I volunteered to clean him myself. I had to taste his sweet nectar and once I did I was hooked. Ever since that night, he's been our man.

As I pulled into the hospital's parking lot, I didn't know what to expect but my sister who I had betrayed and had a whole family with the man she loved was asking me to help her. I feel bad about what happened to Candace and Nakia, but I was not about to help them put my man in jail. I needed him free so he could help take care of our kids. Even though I know it's going to hurt Nakia once she finds out the truth, it won't matter because rather she likes it or not, it happened and I can't take it back. Shit I love him now, so it ain't no going back or nothing. This is one of those it is what it is situations.

Candace had just come out of surgery again and was heavily sedated. They told us we had to wait a couple hours before seeing her because she was in recovery; then we would be able to go back one at a time. I hated hospitals as it is and seeing my girl in that condition had me angry and scared. If you weren't having a baby, nothing else good was happening. If it wasn't for my brother Moe being here, I would have lost it already.

Moe was a real standup guy, watching him talk and try to console Nakia made me smile on the inside because I knew she needed somebody to lean on. I couldn't be much help because I was pissed at her; but in reality, there was nothing she really could have done. Kareem was a man up against two lightweight women.

'Soon as I see this motherfucker I'm going to string his ass up by his ankles and give him that straight grown man ass whipping.' I thought punching my fist into my hand. Ummp...And if this night couldn't get any worse, here come this trifling ass bitch Angela.

"Hey everybody." she greeted with her fake ass.

Moe and Nakia spoke but I had a deep scowl on my face I guess she got the point because she sat down and started asking Nakia questions about what the doctors was saying. I know I probably should have been nicer to

Angela considering the fact that she is my girl's sister and all, but fuck her. It was really hard for me to be fake with people. I think it had a lot to do with my mom and how she raised us to speak our mind as long as we weren't being disrespectful to adults. If it was an adult that did something wrong or said something to hurt our feelings, you best to believe Mama Ann was on they ass. So no I don't feel like compromising my morals for her. Angela was one of those women that couldn't be trusted alone with anybody's man. I hated women like that because I'm a respectable man and a gentleman until you give me a reason not to be; which brings me back to why I don't like Angela.

The year before last, me and Candace decided to throw our twins a big birthday party for their second birthday. We invited all of our friends and family and went all out. We rented bounce houses, snow cone machines, popcorn poppers and more. The kids were having a ball and we were ready to turn up too. Both of our mothers knew we wanted to smoke and take a couple of shots, so after running around playing with the kids for a another hour or so, my mom let us get a break.

"Y'all can go on a smoke break or whatever." she said and I damn near jumped for joy because a nigga was beyond tired. All of us that smoke got up and I lead them to the patio.

"Babe, me and Nakia will go upstairs and roll I'll be back." Candace said then kissed me and walked away with Nakia following closely behind her.

We had already put out extra chairs just for that occasion. I went and grabbed the two bottles of wine out of the fridge and came back. As soon as I opened the door to the patio, I could see Angela trying to push up on Kareem. He was trying to get her off of him but her drunk ass wouldn't take no for an answer. I went over and grabbed her and tried to sit her in a chair but she was resisting. The bitch even tried to kiss me on the lips! Candace and Nakia walked out just as I was trying to mush her face but she was sucking on my tongue making it harder. I saw the hurt on Candace's face, but her being the woman she is, she played it cool to a degree. She grabbed her sister by her hair and snatched her neck back breaking the kiss instantly. She whispered in her ear but I heard every word she said.

"Bitch you better get yourself together before I kill you about mine." Candace warned.

I'm not a cheater and Candace knew that about me. I will be the first to admit that the situation looked bad, but the way she looked at me shook my soul. It took us awhile to recover off of that because it was done in front of friends and family; but from that day on, I vowed to stay away from Angela's whorish ass.

Now to see her over there playing the concerned sister role is making me sick to my stomach. She knows damn well she got a family with her sister's man. The bitch is just trifling.

The nurse walked in breaking my train of disgust and announced that we could she Candace now but one at a time.

Jaquan

By the time I made it back to my place, I
didn't really know what else was left for me to
do. I didn't want Nakia to feel like I had
abandoned her but damn, I still had cases I
needed to work on. I knew she wanted to get her
baby back but her sister needed her help. Well
not really her help, but she needed her to be
there for support. I wondered briefly if Pokey
and Dread had any luck on their end, but I didn't
have their number to call and check. We were
cool but we had one of those relationships where
when we linked up everything was all good but
if we didn't see each other, we didn't talk. I
decided since there was nothing I could do to
help Nakia out, that I'd get back to work so
that's exactly what I did.

I grabbed the case file that's for
Kareem's ole snitching ass. I wanted to beat his
ass so bad and I knew Nakia wouldn't mind; but
my only problem was messing my career up
over a female. He's not one of those niggas that
can leave it in the streets. I think his ass will go
to the cops on me real quick. Well I knew that
for a fact because he didn't have enough drugs
on him to get any more than a possession
charge. He could just plead guilty to that and say
that he uses it then go to rehab for ninety days.
That's a cake walk, but he didn't want to do that.
This man agreed to help catch Zo the Don in
exchange for no time what so ever. His record
would be wiped clean of his traffic tickets and
this one misdemeanor charge, which was all he
had. If I was him, I'd do the rehab and get back

105

out then do my thing. I've known Zo for some years and he's not the one you want to try to set up. I see him from time to time and speak to him, but that's about it.

He's known for having people in his pocket but I didn't want to be one of those people. I wanted to build my name the right way and that's why I steered clear of him.

I read over the case file trying to figure out if I could get Kareem no jail time without him rolling over on Zo. The only reason I was doing that is because Nakia made it clear that she didn't want him dead and Zo would definitely have him killed if word got out that he'd turned snitch.

"Wait a minute!" I said out loud as I read over the undercover's statement. He'd said that Kareem reached into his pocket after he'd agreed to buy a zip so he arrested him.

"You cuffed him too soon buddy." I said out loud with a laugh. I didn't care what kind of pants a nigga wearing he can't fit a zip in his pocket. He had dope in his pocket but it was only enough to prove recreational use.

I ran to my home office and called Mr. Bowers. I knew he was probably having dinner with his wife but I honestly didn't give a damn. I'd found my first break in a case and we'd be able to squash the deal that Mr. Bowers went ahead and put into place thinking he could talk Kareem into signing those papers.

"This better be important you know-"

"It is Mr. Bowers listen. I was reading over casefile 8." I paused to give him time to grab his copy of it. "The undercover officer never saw the zip. From his statement, he cuffed him and took him without reading him his rights. All you have to do is call Kareem and confirm!"

I was beyond excited and I knew Mr. Bowers could tell. He was silent for a few minutes but I knew he was looking over the case to verify that what I was saying was true. I couldn't believe we'd missed it.

"Alright Mr. Miller, I'll call our client right now." he said and I couldn't stop smiling. This was going to be so great for my career. My first case thrown out on a technicality.

"Alright thanks sir. Enjoy your dinner."

"Mr. Miller?" he called out before I could hang the phone up.

"Yes sir?" I answered.

"Good job." he said and my smile grew wider than before. It felt good to not only do a good job but be recognized for it.

"Thank you sir. Good night." I said then hung the phone up.

I was so excited and I had to call someone. I ran to my cell phone and just dialed a number then sat down and waited for them to answer. My body was literally riddled with excitement as if it coursed through my veins instead of blood.

"Hello?" her voice was unsteady but that didn't matter to me at the moment. All I could think about was my case and sharing the great news about my break.

"Man I just caught my first break in a case! I'm well on my way!" I yelled with a voice filled with excitement. This was by far the best thing that had happened to me other than running into Nakia again.

"Aw baby that's good! I'm happy for you!" she cheered but all of my excitement went away. I felt so bad for calling Miko, so I just hung the phone up.

How could I get Nakia in my life full time if I was still stuck on Miko? I didn't really think I was stuck but damn, what reason did I have for calling her instead of Nakia? I tried to correct what I'd done by calling Nakia so I could see how things were at the hospital with her sister. I knew things had to be bad for her to stop looking for her baby to go see her, but she didn't answer her phone. I sighed heavily and just went back to my desk to start on another case.

Miko

"Why are you looking like that now?" my mom asked with a look of frustration on her face. I could tell my drama was getting on her nerves by her tone of voice but that look that she was giving me confirmed it.

"That was Jaquan." I said to her but she just rolled her eyes. She was dead set on me marrying Christian even after he came over here and broke her fucking door.

"What I tell you about losing a good man Miko?" she asked with both hands on her hips. I knew she was about to go into a rant and I didn't want to hear it but I knew that if I stopped her, she'd make me go home to Christian and I didn't want that even more. "I've taught you everything that I know. This luxurious house you like to come lounge around in is paid for and in my name. Baby you can have all of this if you just listen to me." she said and I looked around her beautiful home.

"Mama I just want to be happy." I responded sadly. At first I loved the gifts that fucking different men got me and all of the nuts that I could get but once I got a taste of Jaquan then lost him, everything that I wanted changed.

"Girl you sound foolish." she said with a frown on her face as shook her head. "Happiness comes from within! All you need is you to be happy! Let Christian take care of you and you will be set for life." she said as she sat down beside me.

"Ma you don't understand. I don't want any of this if I can't have Jaquan. He's all I want."

"He's all I want." she mocked me in a whiny childlike voice.

I knew I didn't sound like that but I also knew that this conversation was going nowhere. I picked my phone up so I could call him back but she knocked the phone out of my hand.

"Ma!" I whined with a deep frown on my face.

I was trying not to cry because my life was literally falling apart right before my very eyes and it all happened because I'd been listening to my mom my whole life. Every decision that I made was due to her influence in some type of way except the one I was about to make about choosing the man that I loved.

"Don't Ma me little girl. You need to pull yourself together then go home to your man. You have a professional baseball player on your hand and you want a nigga barely making ends meet? Is you dumb or is you stupid?"

I rolled my eyes then sat back against the couch completely frustrated. My phone vibrated on the floor and when I looked down at it, Christian's name displayed across the screen. I contemplated answering it just so I could tell him to leave me alone, but I decided against it. My mom looked between me and the phone but I knew she wasn't going to answer it. Christian crossed a major line when he broke my mom's door and it let me know that he can get violent. My mouth's too slick to be with someone that may hit me in the future just because he didn't get his way.

"Give him time to think about what he's done but you're going back home to him." my mom said as if she could read my mind. I guess she didn't care if he beat me just as long as he had some money to buy the makeup I would need to cover it up.

"I hear ya ma." I said as I stood to my feet and walked to the bathroom.

My body was so tense, so I wanted to take a long hot bath. I ran nothing but hot water and lit vanilla candles around the outside of the tub. Then I poured bath beads in the water to make it feel silky. I sighed heavily as I undressed then eased my body into the tub slowly. I used my foot to switch on the jets that massage your bottom and back by shooting water recycled from the tub at you. The pressure felt so good between my legs and I didn't want to move.

"Am I a nympho?" I asked myself softly. I pulled my bottom lip into my mouth as I thought about Jaquan. I'd had sex with Christian and Casamoney both today and I wondered if I'd be pushing it if I popped up at Jaquan's house.

Thirty more minutes into my soak and I felt brand new. The water was warm now so I let it out then stepped out of the tub. I dried my body off, put lotion on then walked to my room naked. Jaquan loved it when I wore sweatpants and a form fitting muscle shirt for women. He said he loved how my small titties sat up with no bra and he loved the fact that I never wore panties even more.

I slipped my feet into some flip flops then headed back upfront. My mom was in the kitchen singing along to her music so I knew she wouldn't realize that I was gone until it was too late. I gripped my keys tight in my hand so she wouldn't hear them, then grabbed my phone and made my way out of the door quietly. My car was new so I knew she wouldn't hear it crank; so once I was in the car, I was free to go.

With thoughts of Jaquan heavy on my mind, I played a song that we listened to the very first time that we had sex all of those years ago. It was my go to song whenever he was upset with me and I was using sex to fix it. The smooth melody soothed my soul but made my body yearn for his as I listened to the lyrics of the song and drove down the street. My mind took me back to that very day. I knew I had to seal the deal fast because Angela had just told me that her sister Nakia had a huge crush on him.

"Hey Angie what's up?"

I'd called her on the phone to see if Nakia had made her move on him or not yet. If she hadn't, then I was going to invite him over while my mom was out on a date.

"Nothing who is this?" she asked dryly and I just rolled my eyes.

Anytime I've talked to her in person, she would be all in my face and shit but now she was acting like she didn't know my voice.

"It's Miko. I was calling to see if Nakia told Jaquan how she felt yet." I held my breath in anticipation of her answer.

"No, go for it." she said and I hung the phone up.

I decided to skip the rest of our conversation so I could call Jaquan and invite him over. Once he told me that he was going to walk to my house right then, I ran to my mom's bathroom and took a shower. I used her lotion to lotion up with then borrowed her Xscape CD because I'd heard her play it whenever she had company. I waited patiently for Jaquan to arrive and when he did, I took him straight in my room and pressed play on my favorite song.

"It's a glowing little feeling,
Like a summer sun that slowly rises,
On a new horizon of love"

I gently pulled his bottom lip into my mouth like I'd seen someone do on a movie. We kissed softly at first.

"And it's more exotic than Jamaica,
Or the rain that falls in Costa Rica,
Like a waterfall to the sea,"

His hands roamed all over my body as I pulled my pajama pants and panties off. I broke our kiss just long enough to take my shirt off then I kissed him again.

"So tell me baby
Do you want to fly, I can take you high,
Come ride on these midnight skies.
If you're looking for Heaven's only door,
You've got the key baby open me."

He stepped out of his pants then laid my body gently on the bed. My pussy felt like it had a heart beat as he rubbed his hard dark against it while we were kissing.

"Baby won't you come inside,
I'll take you on a fantasy ride.
Take a journey through my universe,
My love's the softest place on earth."

A sharp gasp escaped from my mouth when he'd finally stuck the head of his dick inside of me. I'd had sex before but it never felt like that. He went in slowly inch by inch.

"You don't have to pull the blinds,
Let the neighbors lose their minds.

Baby you can be the first,
Inside the softest place on earth."

      I moaned softly as I wrapped my legs around his waist. I'd felt many types of pleasure but nothing quite like this before. As he slid in and out of me slowly with his eyes closed tight, I knew I could never let him go.

"Overflowing with emotion,
I can make you feel so sensual,
When I touch you, you will lose all control."

      I flipped him over and slid down his dick slowly. I'd never ridden a dick before but I'd watched this movie that said it was just like riding a horse. Up, down, back, forth, faster, faster. He closed his eyes again but I leaned my body over and kissed his lips.

"Come on baby, kiss me all over,
From my mountains to my valley low,
There's an ocean of love just for you,
Just for you."

      His breathing quickened so I slowed my pace until I was sitting completely still. He leaned up and pulled one of my nipples into his mouth and I moaned out in pure pleasure.

"Do you want to fly, I can take you high,
Come ride on these midnight skies.
If you're looking for heaven's only door,
You've got the key baby open me."

He tried to pick me up so he could flip me back over but he lost his balance and we both hit the floor. The radio fell off of the dresser and hit the floor but the music didn't stop. Well not completely anyway. It skipped over and over again. And we just laughed.

BEEEEEEEPPPP!

The sound of a car horn blaring at me snapped me back to the reality that I was driving and had just ran a red light. One hand flew to my chest as I looked back at the car that had just barely missed me. My heart was beating out of control but my pussy was wet due to my vivid memory. I looked around expecting the police to come after me but nobody came, so I headed straight to Jaquan's house to try to get him back one last time.

<u>Christian</u>

When I called Miko I just wanted to apologize but she didn't answer the phone. I didn't know what else to do so I called my brother Jeremiah to get some advice from him. I use to call Jaquan whenever we had problems, but that was before he knew we were seeing the same girl.

"You called off the wedding yet?" Jeremiah answered his phone asking. He knew exactly how I felt about Miko so I had no idea why he thought I was going to call off the wedding.

"Naw bruh, but I fucked up! I went to her mom's house and shit got a little heated. I broke the glass door and-"

"Wa, wait, wait a minute man! You broke a glass door at her mama house?! Nigga you bugging forreal! If the pussy that good nigga I don't ever want to sample it." he said and I felt some type of way about the fact that sampling my fiance's pussy ever crossed his mind.

"Nigga don't worry about my girl pussy!"

"That goes without saying for me bruh. Jaquan should have been telling your ass that though." he said and I sighed heavily. I didn't call him to get into it with him so it was best that I go ahead and end the argument.

"I didn't call to argue man. I don't know how to fix this." I said honestly as I hit block after block. I was lost in my own thoughts as I drove around in circles.

"Replace the door and call off the wedding. I don't know why you want to marry a bitch you took from your cousin any fucking way." Jeremiah said and I could imagine him shaking his head at me.

"Man I'm gone replace the door then I'mma marry her. Thanks for the chat." I said sarcastically then hung the phone up in his face. I didn't have time for him to be judging what I did. Shit I knew it was wrong but I was about to make an honest woman out of her.

I decided to head back to her mom's house so I could try to talk her into coming back home. I ended up taking the wrong exit and it took an extra thirty minutes to make it to her mom's house. As soon as I got to the intersection by her mom's house, I saw someone drive straight through a red light and almost get hit by another car. Before I could say anything crazy about what I'd seen, I realized that that was Miko's car. I hopped over into the other lane so I could turn off and follow her just as soon as it was safe to do so. I wondered what was going on that would make her do such a stupid thing like she'd just done. She was normally a pretty good, safe driver so I knew it had to have been an emergency. I followed her so I could be there in case she needed me. I didn't know if someone was hurt or not but I was going to be there for moral support.

When she took an exit that was familiar to me, my blood started to boil almost instantly but I knew I had to be mistaken. After all, it had been a really long time since I've been to Jaquan's house. I called her phone to see if she would answer and just as I suspected, she didn't. I watched her pick it up and look at it then put it back down. I didn't know what to do, what to say or what to think at this point. When she turned on his street, I stayed a few houses down and watched her park in his yard like she still lived there. I called her again when she got out of the car and surprisingly, she answered the phone.

"What Christian?" she stood in the middle of the driveway and answered the phone. I wondered why she didn't keep walking if this was an innocent trip.

"Where you at? I want to see you." I said even though I knew she was still mad at me. That didn't give her the right to go sleep with my best friend though!

"Where do you think I am? You know what Christian, I'm tired of arguing with you. Just leave me alone." she said and disconnected the call. I tried to call her back but it went straight to voicemail, so I knew she'd powered it off.

My fucking heart dropped down in my stomach when she used her key to get in. She told me that she'd given him his key back but she'd lied. But why hadn't he changed the locks? He had to still want her there and that wasn't cool with me at all. I debated on rather or not I should get out of the car and knock on the door but I figured I'd wait a few minutes so I could catch them in the act. I didn't have a key but I knew my brother did, so I called him back to see if he could bring it to me.

"What's up?" he answered the phone and I could hear his baby mama talking in the background. He didn't like Miko and I didn't like her, so I guess we're finally even.

"I need you to bring Jaquan's key to me. I'm outside of his house."
"Wait, what? What the fuck bruh? Why you outside his house and why do you need his key? Is he home?" he fired off one question after the other one.

"Man listen, I just followed Miko to his house and now she's inside. I need to go in and stop them." I said quickly and he started laughing at me. He laughed so hard that I pulled the phone away from my ear and still heard him.

"Man I ain't getting in y'all shit." he said then hung the phone up. I sighed heavily because I had no choice but to get out and knock on the door.

Kareem

I've been a nervous fucking wreck since Miko left because I know she was fucking with that nigga Jaquan. If that bitch told him where we were, I was going to beat the fuck out of her. Once again I was thinking with my dick. Miko had some good ass pussy but nobody's pussy felt better than Nakia. Her shit was tight, wet, warm and it gripped my dick tighter than my fist when I'm jacking off! I loved that girl with every breath in my body but it was just too many bitches for me to settle down right now. I've been having babies on her, but it wasn't intentional. A nigga just wasn't trying not to.

I really fucked up when I got Angela pregnant twice, but she ain't say nothing. Our son looks just like Amberia did as a baby but Nakia never pays those kids any attention and I know it's because she doesn't fuck with their mom. I'm just glad Angela hasn't told her yet because I want to be the one to tell her. I only have seven kids though, and I'm getting snipped as soon as possible because I can't keep doing this to her. She only knows about one child and I almost lost her over that. I can't handle not having her in my life. She cooks, cleans and holds a nigga down the way everybody need their woman to, but she's boring. She never wants to go out with me and that's where I always meet these other bitches at. I know it's not right but shit, she's wrong for never wanting to come with me. If she was there, I wouldn't be worried about them bitches because I'd have her with me.

I walked in the bathroom to take a piss and the shit hurt like hell. My dick been hurting when I piss for about two weeks now and it was getting worse. I even had a little red color in my urine. Nakia hadn't said anything to me about nothing so I guess I don't have nothing, but then again I haven't fucked her in about a month. She knows I been in these streets heavy so she haven't been putting out.

I looked myself in the mirror and tried to figure out who I could have gotten something from if I have something but I kept drawing a blank. Shit I'd have to do a roll call like DMX did on that song when he was like:

"There was Brenda, Latisha, Linda, Felicia
Dawn, LeShaun, Ines and Alicia
Teresa, Monica, Sharron, Nicki
Lisa, Veronica, Karen, Vicky
Cookie, well I met her in a ice cream parlor
Tonya, Diane, Lori and Carla
Marina, Selena, Katrina, Sabrina
About three Kim's, Latoya and Tina
Shelley, Bridget, Cavi, Rasheeda
Kelly, Nicole, Angel, Juanita
Stacy, Tracie, Rohna and Ronda
Donna, Ulanda, Tawana and Wanda"

Shit I probably hit more bitches than that in the last month. I been leaning and rolling a lot so I can't be too sure. I washed my hands then headed back in the room with my daughter.

"Daddy I want mommy." Amberia said with tears streaming down her cheeks. She'd been complaining about her head hurting but she keeps falling asleep, so it must not be hurting too bad.

"Later baby." I said just as my phone started ringing again. Everybody had been blowing me up but this time it was somebody that I actually wanted to talk to.

"Hey Mr. Bowers. How you doing?" I asked because the last time we spoke, he was having an EKG done because of some chest pains he'd been having.

"I'm doing just fine young man. Look I have a question. When you were arrested, did he read you your rights?" he asked and I thought about it for a few seconds so I wouldn't be lying.

I remember going in my pocket but he grabbed my arm and pushed me to the ground and slammed the cuffs on me. I tried to speak but he told me to shut up and threw me in the back of his car.

"Man I'll tell on anybody you need man I'm just a little fish but I can give you the big ones." I lied as soon as they came in the interrogation room with me.

I'd already been booked so I didn't know why they put me in the interrogation room anyway. I figured they wanted to cut a deal and I wanted to get out of jail so I cooperated.

"Naw, he didn't." I said once I replayed the events of that night in my head. I knew it had to be good news or he wouldn't call me this time of night.

"Listen, we're gonna have your case thrown out because of that fact alone and you have my prodigy Jaquan Miller to thank for that! Hopefully he'll be taking over my company once I retire next fall." Mr. Bowers said and my mouth fell wide open in disbelief.

"I'll be sure to thank him and thank you as well Mr. Bowers. Good night." I said then hung the phone up.

I wondered why he'd went out of his way to help me. I hope he didn't think that I was going to let him have my girl just because he found me a get out of jail free card.

"Maybe he just wants Amberia back." I said outloud as I used my phone to text Nakia. I knew she had her whole family out looking for me by now so I was just going to take Amberia home and leave her there then text Nakia and tell her.

Nakia

"Nakia!" Sly barked and it scared the shit out of me as he entered back into the waiting room. I jumped up from the chair that I was sitting in to meet him halfway. From his tone and facial expression, I feared the worst.

"What's wrong?" I asked frantically. My nerves were already bad because I didn't know where my daughter was so they were really shot at that moment.

"Candace is asking for you." he replied.

I sighed heavily because if she can ask for me then she's doing better. I didn't waste any time asking questions as I reached down to grab my purse and scrambled down the hallway. I arrived in front of the door with her name on it and started to have second thoughts. I didn't know what to expect once I opened the door but whatever I saw, I knew it was partially my fault. We all knew Kareem had a little temper, but I never thought he would go this far to put his hands on one of us. I let out a deep breath that I hadn't realized I was holding until I released it and pushed the door open.

"Hey sissy pooh." I said as I forced a smile. It was like her face lit up when she saw me and it let me know that there was no love lost.

"Ouch!" Candace screamed out in pain as she attempted to sit up. I could tell how much pain she was in by the look on her face.

"No sis lay back and try to relax. You don't have to sit up for me." I informed her as I walked over to her bed to fluff her pillows and make her more comfortable.

"Thank you sis." Candace said as she reached out and grabbed my hand.

I kissed her cheek then assured her that it not a problem at all but for some reason, she wouldn't turn my hand loose. I looked into her face I could tell immediately that she was weak and in more pain. It tore my soul up to see my sister in this condition and her only fault was trying to protect me and my daughter.

"Nakia sit down. I need to tell you something." Candace said in a low voice.

"Um, okay is everything okay?" I asked as I pulled a chair up to her hospital bed. My leg started to shake as my nerves kicked into overdrive. I knew from her tone that she wasn't about to tell me something good.

"After this incident, it made me realize that life is too short and tomorrow is not promised. I love you and I hope you can forgive me for keeping this secret." she began and my heart dropped down into the pit of my stomach.

Candace and I never kept things from each other so naturally I assumed it was the medicine. It's what I wanted to believe that it was so I giggled at her until she spoke up again.

"Kareem and Angela are sleeping together." she said as she stared deep into my eyes. "Demarious is his son." she continued and I just stared at her for several seconds before I started laughing.

"Okay sis, now I know it's the medicine. Maybe you should try and get some sleep because you talking crazy right now." I said in a shaky voice. I was pretending to be stronger than I actually was.

She grabbed my hand again but this time tighter than before. "I am serious Nakia. Wake up sis and see what's right in front of your face. I'm telling you because according to what my friend said, they are about to have another one."

I felt like all of the breath in my body had been taken away from me. I slid back in the chair to think about what Candace was saying to me. My head was spinning and my stomach turned upside down just thinking about my sister and my man sleeping together.

There is no way this could be true because Angela and Kareem hated each other.

"Candace I need you to be one hundred percent sure about what you are saying before I reign hell and brimstone on them two." I said with rage that was quickly replaced with sadness. "And why didn't you say something sooner?"

"Because I didn't want to see you hurt like you are right now. I'm so sorry Nakia that I betrayed you." she paused and swallowed hard. I knew she could feel the pain as it radiated from my body. "I just wanted to keep our family together. We are not perfect but we are blood and I love all of y'all.

"I am going to beat Angela's ass!" I told Candace.

"No sis, it's not the time for that. I want you to see for yourself. What's done in the dark will always come to light." she continued saying what our mama always said.

"When the time is right we will confront them together and go from there because they will never tell truth if you ask." she continued but I just couldn't believe what I'd just heard.

I sat in silence for the next ten minutes. My heart felt like it was bursting at the seams as the tears rolled down my face. I knew Casamoney was not faithful but I never thought he would stoop low enough to fuck my sister and have a child, maybe two.

"Well you have other people waiting to visit you so I'm going to get on outta here. I have some things to do so I will be back tomorrow." I told Candace before I kissed her cheek goodbye.

"Nakia just concentrate on finding my niece. She is all that matters right now."

Candace said to me. She was right, but that didn't make me want to fuck Angela up any less.

I nodded my head in agreement because I could live without any man but couldn't survive a day without Amberia. Angela and Kareem would both get theirs, real soon too.

Before I could exit the room, my text message alert went off. I reached in my jacket pocket to see who it was. I didn't have time for random conversations but when I saw who it was, my eyes got big as saucers.

Kareem: Go home 911

After I read that message, I took running and didn't stop until I was outside. I flagged down a cabbie driver that was waiting on a fare and jumped inside without asking any questions.

"1735 Plaza Lane and please hurry!" I rushed out in a panic. I prayed all the way there that nothing had happened to my child. I wanted to call Jaquan but after overhearing him and Miko having sex, I was done with him.

As soon as the cab turned on my street, I felt a little relieved because I didn't hear any sirens or see no police. I didn't even give the cab driver time to pull in the driveway before I tossed two twenties across the front seat and jumped out running. I knew somebody was there because the light in my room and Amberia's room were on. I never leave lights on in my house when I'm not there. *'My baby!'* I thought as I ran up the driveway with my shoes in my hand. I felt around in my purse for my house keys but hands were shaking so hard that I kept dropping them. Finally, I was able to unlock the door and run inside. The rest of the house was dark so I ran upstairs.

"AMBERIA!" I screamed but got no response.

"KAREEM!" I screamed but still got no response.

I got to my room first and saw that a lot of things were missing. The dresser drawers and closets were open. I walked in and closed them and that's when I saw it. There was a letter on the dresser and I grabbed it before I ran to Amberia's room. I had to check and see if her things were still there. I turned the knob and opened her door and there she was asleep with her sippy cup. I ran to the bed and picked her up. I hugged her so tight and kissed her chubby cheeks but something wasn't right. She opened her eyes but kept falling back to sleep.
I knew from the knot on her head that she probably had a concussion and needed medical attention.

"Shit, I don't have my car!" I screamed. With Amberia in my arms, I tried to keep her awake but it wasn't working. "Oh God, help me!" I know it was wishful thinking but I looked out the window to see if the cab was still there, it wasn't.

"Okay baby, you are going to be okay." I said as I picked up the house phone and dialed 911. The operator came on and ask me to hold. "No I cannot hold!" I screamed in the phone but no one was there. I took out my cell and called Jaquan maybe he could help but I got his voicemail so I left a message.

"911 what's your emergency?" The operator asked once I called back.

I wanted to curse her ass out but now wasn't the time. I needed to get my baby to the hospital and quickly. I explained her condition and she informed me that the ambulance was on the way. I called my brothers but they weren't answering either. *'What the fuck is going on?'* I thought to myself. Let me call Sly. When he answered, I was relieved that somebody had answered so I could tell them what was going on. I told him I would keep him updated once I heard the paramedics at the door.

While they checked on Amberia, I gathered up her cup and toys and a change of clothes. I ran in my room to get my purse and remembered the letter so I stuck it in my purse and got in the ambulance with my daughter. I couldn't believe Kareem just left her like that. She could have died if she fell into a deep sleep. I promise if it's with my last breath, he is going to pay for this shit.

Soon as we got to Hughes Spalding Children's hospital, they rushed her to the back to triage her and run test. The nurse sat me in a room to wait for Amberia to come back. I was a nervous wreck. As I looked through my purse for some gum, I pulled out the now crumpled up letter and began to read it.

Dear Nakia,

I know you are mad at me but please understand that I didn't mean for none of this to happen. It's just that seeing you with that nigga Jaquan set me off. I know it's hard to believe what I say because I have lied and hurt you so much but I truly do love you and my daughter and want to be a family.

I took my things and left because I know you need time to calm down, but please know that I will never let you go. Whatever you and dude got going on dead it. You are mines and I'm coming back for what belongs to me.

Amberia is in her room ma. I know you would lose your mind without her and she loves you too. Please tell Candace that I'm sorry, I just lost my head. I'll see y'all soon. I love you Nakia and I'm sorry for hurting you again.
Casamoney

Angela

"You need to mind your damn business!" I shouted at Sly.

His ass was really working my last fucking nerves and it was taking everything in me not snap completely out. Out of nowhere, Nakia came running past the waiting room as if her ass was on fire. She didn't say a word to anybody, no goodbye, no see you later, nothing. It wasn't like I cared, but it was rude as fuck considering she called me for support. Okay, maybe I'm being a bit selfish because Candace is my sister too and I did want to be here for her. I sure as hell didn't need this drama that Sly was spitting though.

"Man I know you know where Casamoney at. Just tell me now and I won't kill him." Sly continued even though I'd already told his ass that I didn't know where he was.

"Boy please. If you don't get the fuck out my face and more importantly out my business, we gone a major misunderstanding." I snapped right back at him. It was like the more he talked the more pissed off I got, but it was because I really didn't know where he was.

"Look I'm going to see my sister since Speedy Gonzales is gone." I informed Sly then walked away.

I swear I couldn't stand him anymore. I can't believe I ever wanted to give him some of my pussy. Let me stop lying, that nigga fine as hell; and even though I'm pregnant by Casamoney, if he asked nicely I'd give it to him too. A slight chill went down my spine at the thought of how good that dick would be right before going in my sister's room.

I spent about an hour visiting with Candace. I didn't leave until I couldn't take her saying one more word about my baby daddy, what he did to her, or how I was wrong by betraying my sister like that. Blahh, Blahh, Blahh. I felt like I was listening to Rich homie Quan.

"I feel you sis but with all due respect, this is my life and I love Casamoney. We are going to be together no matter what none of y'all think." I paused and stared at her for several seconds. "So did you tell her?" I asked because deep down inside, I wanted her too. It was time for Nakia to come off her high horse and let my man be free.

"No." Candace finally answered before falling back asleep.

I kissed her forehead and left. When I got in my car, I guess what everybody was saying was weighing hard on me because I couldn't stop thinking about Casamoney and the life we have together. I picked up my cell phone to call him again. After I thought about it for a minute I decided to text him this time.

Angela: Where you at? I need to see you.

Big Daddy: Why? What's up?

Angela: Just missing you and need some dick.

Big Daddy: No doubt, I know you heard what happened, so I'm laying low until it boils over.

Angela: How long? It's been two weeks since we've seen you.

Big Daddy: You knew what you were getting into, so don't start tripping!! I will send you money by Mario.

Angela: We need you, come home.

Big Daddy: I'm trying, she won't let me. Goodnight Angela.

My feelings were really hurt after Casamoney's last text. Here I was defending our relationship and now he's treating me like some truck stop whore. I cried all the way to the house. I hope that he wasn't thinking about leaving me and my kids to go back to Nakia or some other random bitch. We supposed to be in love and getting married. I know the feelings that I have for him are mutual or he wouldn't have gotten me pregnant again. I mean one time may be considered a mistake, but not two times. He'd made a conscious decision not to strap up and he knew that I don't like being on birth control and he still came all inside of me. He didn't care about Nakia when he was beating this pussy up, but now he wants to act like he cares about her!

I was so mad that when I parked my car outside of my home, I punched the steering wheel over and over again. If he thought he was going to play with my heart without consequences then he had better think again. I'm going to tell Nakia myself and she'll never be with him again. If I'm lucky, her ass won't talk to me anymore either, because I really don't like the bitch.

Candace

"No don't kill him!" I screamed. I was running so fast even though everything in my body hurt.

"Babe wake up! You having a nightmare." I heard my fiance Sly say as he gently shook my shoulder.

"Damn, it felt so real." I told him as I wiped the slob off my mouth. "Yeah I know not a pretty sight." I giggled with Sly.

"Are you okay babe?" he asked as he looked at me with worry lines on his forehead. I smiled at him then reached out for his hand.

"Yes, I'm just afraid of how all this drama is going to turn out." I confessed. I knew everyone involved on our side wanted to kill Kareem but I also knew that Nakia wouldn't want that.

From the look on Sly's face, I could tell he had his concerns too.

"Look babe. Real talk, as long as you and our kids are okay." he paused like he was choosing his words carefully. "I say let the chips fall where they may. I know them are your sisters and you want the best for them, but this is their mess to deal with. You trying to help landed you up in here away from your own kids." Sly stated as he shook his head.

I thought about what he said as I laid there staring at the T.V. We don't lay down for shit, especially when one of us gets hurt; and in this, case a child was taken.

I knew what Sly was trying to do. He was damn near begging me to let my brothers and him handle it, but there was no way I was going to stay out of this one. I also knew he wasn't going to help me get my revenge though. Sly knew better than anybody that my fight game was on one hundred and I could shoot just as well because he'd taught me; and still for some reason, every time some drama went down, he treated me like a lame or a defenseless ass child. We been fighting all our lives, I didn't need his permission to be me.

Don't get me wrong, Sly is the love of my life and I respect him, but he has to learn that I'm a big girl. He just going to have to understand that this was family and with or without his help, I was not going to let them down.

"Knock! Knock!" Someone said before peeking their head the door. "Mrs. Willis how are you feeling? I'm Dr. Leslie. I was the one who performed your surgeries."

"I'm good Dr. Leslie. This is my fiance Sabago." I introduced them.

After giving me a quick exam, he told me everything looked okay and I would probably be able to go home tomorrow if I promised to take it easy. I promised.

A few minutes after the doctor left, Sly told me he had to get going because he was trying to close the deal on his club with the Jamaicans. I was so proud of my baby for trying to go legit. He was really working hard to get out of these streets. He kissed me goodnight so passionately that it made me dizzy and I was ready to rip the clothes off my sexy man. We both had business to attend to and the sooner he left, the faster I could get started on mines so I let him leave.

"I will be here early in the morning to pick you up." he stated then winked at me and left the room.

He didn't know what time I would be discharged while he's telling me when he's coming back. I reached into the nightstand table and grabbed my iPhone to call my one go to dude, Mason.

Mason

I was driving down Hwy 78 heading home deep in thought about my life, my kids and the mistakes that I've made when my cell phone rang, jarring me out of my thoughts. A smile immediately graced my face when I glanced down and saw a picture of Candace pop up. It was a selfie she took in the mirror showing off her new Brazilian hair. Her skin was flawless and them hazel eyes still have me mesmerized. *'Three kids later and she still fine as hell.'* I thought right before I hit my Bluetooth.

"Hey little lady, how are you feeling?" I questioned because I was worried about her. The only reason that I wasn't at the hospital with her was out of respect for her and her relationship.

"I'm sore as hell from the broken ribs, but I'll live. How is my baby?" She asked referring to Jayceon, our son.

"He good, knocked out in the back seat. We did a little shopping and caught a movie." I informed her because she is very involved in her children's life.

It doesn't matter who they were with, she's calling and checking on them, getting on your damn nerves. If they tell her anything crazy she coming to see what's up.

"I'm glad y'all had a good time. At least I know he did because that's the only time he's asleep this early." she said with a little giggle.

"But look Mason, I really called to ask a favor of you."

"Of course! Anything for you, what's up?" I asked.

"I want Kareem to pay for what he did to me and since he trying to ruin my family, I want to get him both physically and financially," she said and I could hear the vengeance in her voice.

"Oh Mercy, somebody done woke up Mrs. Troublemaker!" I laughed but something told me this wouldn't be funny at all to the person involved.

Candace is a computer genius. A lot of people don't know that about her but I have seen her fuck up somebody's whole world with just a few keystrokes. I had the baddest muscle and weapons in the city, so she know whatever she needed, I got it.

"Let me guess, hubby don't approve or he don't know." I just threw that out there.

"A little of both. I'll call you when my plan is together. Oh and thank you baby daddy." she purred before hanging up.

I laughed and shook my head at her. That girl right there is my one that got away. Candace was everything I ever wanted and needed in my life. She's smart, beautiful, talented, loving, loyal and faithful. All the things guys wish for today, I had it with her but I couldn't leave the lifestyle I loved back then; and she wasn't going to settle for my foolishness. I respected her more for walking away and taking my son with her. If she hadn't, he would probably end up just like his brother, doing time in the penitentiary.

I looked in my rearview mirror at Jayceon sleeping so peacefully. It warmed my heart because he was the one that was going to turn out right. I know I won't be around to see it, but I know he was going to turn out to be somebody great.

I busied myself by moving on to my next casefile. As I read through it, I didn't believe any of the evidence against my client. Her name is Rebecca Fields and she's accused of killing her husband. According to the courts, he wanted a divorce and they're trying to say that she couldn't live without him. They got into an argument so she killed him and got rid of the body. The problem with that is, they had nothing to back it up. It was just a theory. She's currently locked up because she's considered a flight risk but she keeps saying that she's innocent. Mr. Bowers said that they all say that rather are or not but I believed her.

All of the evidence the state had against her was circumstantial at best. Unfortunately for her, all they had to be able to do was make the jury believe that it was possible for her to be indicted. I looked at the crime scene photos and noticed the blood splatter looked a bit off. It was suspected that she shot him and then got rid of body, but the blood splatter didn't match any gun that I'd ever seen. It actually looked like it could have been staged. Another thing that threw me off was the fact that a bullet was lodged in the wall, but the blood splatter doesn't look like the victim was standing anywhere near the wall; so how did the bullet get there? The shell casing was found under her couch but it's normal for those to roll a bit, so I understood that part.

"I'm going to get you out Rebecca." I said out loud as if she could hear me in jail.

I checked my calendar to see when I'd be able to take a trip upstate so she and I could discuss some things about her case. I played the tape recorder's recording of our last conversation.

"Mrs. Fields-"

"Ms. Fields." she corrected me and I remembered briefly how embarrassed and caught off guard I was, but neither she nor Mr. Bowers could tell.

"My apologies. Anyway, tell me again what happened the day your husband went missing." I needed clarification.

"I've told you a dozen times." she sighed heavily. "I was working late like I had to do every Thursday, but I made it home earlier than usual. When I got home, he was gone but the blood was there. I couldn't stomach seeing it and had to go throw up. I heard a door close, so I called the police from the bathroom. Once the police arrived, there was no evidence that anyone had been there other than myself and him."

I hit rewind and listened again before it played all the way through. The way she corrected me threw me off. I hit rewind again so I could listen to her tone of voice. She had a serious attitude when she corrected me.

"He had another woman." I said out loud like a light bulb cut on.

The only problem with her knowing that is that it can be used against her. If there is any evidence of her knowing about another woman, I'd have to turn it in and I was sure they would say that it was motive. I knew I had to tread lightly. I began to make notes simply with questions that I needed to ask her when I go see her but was distracted by the sound of my front door opening. *'Who could that be?'* I thought to myself.

I jumped up from my desk then ran out into the hallway and there stood Miko. She smiled at me and began to remove her clothes. I hadn't seen her since the party that Christian announced their engagement at, so I didn't know how to feel at this moment. To make matters even worse, I hadn't had sex or jacked off since the last time that I had sex with her. Nothing had changed about her body and in all honesty, my mouth watered.

"Why are you here?" I asked her as she stood before me naked as the day that she was born. I didn't know what else to say or do so I had to start somewhere.

"I need to feel you." she moaned as she slipped her index finger in her mouth then trailed her thumb down between her legs.

I could feel my dick hardening at the sight before me. She was really putting on a show and if I told you I wasn't enjoying it, then I'd be lying. As bad as she wanted to feel me, I wanted to feel her too. I needed to feel her.

"You need to leave." I croaked out hoarsely because that isn't what I really wanted to happen.

I wanted nothing more than to bend her over and fuck the shit out of her. She smiled at me then squat down on the floor. She looked so sexy and she'd always been so spontaneous when it came down to sex.

"You don't really want that now do you?" she asked as she spread her legs slowly and circled her clit with her index finger. She moaned softly but what got me was the fact that she stared at me the whole time as she played in her pussy.

"No." I admitted as I took a step towards her.

I was nervous as fuck but I'd been a little stressed out lately, so I have some pressure built up. She smiled at me as I made my way to her slowly. She circled her finger around her clit faster and faster. My dick was so hard that it was throbbing against my pants. She's always had this undeniable sex appeal about her and I was ready to fuck her one last time.

Kareem

I wasn't really sure what had gotten into Angela but she's been more clingy than usual now. She knew I was in a relationship from the very beginning and she's the one who wanted me. Now she's acting stupid.

A nigga don't cheat to fall in love. Nakia is about as close to perfect as it gets but she expects too much from me. Then when she doesn't get her way, she nags and nags and nags. I cheat for peace. At one point, I could call Angela at any given time and could swing through, pipe her down and keep it moving. Shit, I used to go months without talking to her and didn't hear a peep out of her. Now it's only been two weeks and the bitch tripping. If I wanted to get nagged all the time I'd just stay my black ass at home. I shook my head as I drove around in circles.

I knew I needed to get somewhere and lay low but I really didn't know where to go. There's this chick named Tina who's a really sweet girl and I've only showed her a good side of me. *'Maybe she'll let me crash at her place.'* I thought to myself. I headed straight there and blew the horn once I was outside. She opened her front door with a frown on her face until she saw that it was me. She ran over to my car, opened the door and gave me a hug.

"I've missed you." she said then kissed me on the cheek. "Hold on let me open the garage." she said then ran back into the house. A few minutes later, the garage door raised slowly and I drove in.

As soon as I made it in her house, the smell of Fabuloso filled my nostrils. Just like every time I'd come over here, she had just got done cleaning up. She doesn't have any kids and she's hardly home so you would think she wouldn't clean up as much as she does, but she's always cleaning.

"What you doing baby?" I asked as she walked towards the back of the house. I took a moment and looked around the living room. It smelled so good and everything was in place.

"I'm about to light these incense." she tossed over her shoulder. I nodded my head even though she couldn't see me then made my way into the living room and took a seat.

"She said when she needs some sexual healing. She said that's when she calls me. She said she never catch no feelings. She said she just wants a plan b." my phone rang out loud in my pocket and I knew who it was before I pulled it out and hit decline. That song is called She said by Young Fox and it fit our situation perfectly, so I had to assign that ringtone to her. There was no other side chick that bugged me as much as she did.

"What was that?" Tina walked up front and asked as she stuck the end of the incense in the wall.

"Pandora started playing." I lied because she had no idea that I was dating anyone but she knew that I have children. She nodded her head and took a seat on the couch.

I wondered why she sat so far away when she normally sits under me but she wasn't talking and I welcomed the quiet. She watched a show on Netflix until her phone started ringing. I glanced over at her as she fumbled nervously and dropped it but the number wasn't programmed in her phone.

"Dammit." she said as she leaned over and picked it up then looked at me. "Can I?" she asked and I nodded my head.

"Hello?" she answered and I couldn't help but feel like the man of the year. She'd just asked for permission to answer her own phone just because I was sitting right here.

"Oh hey! How are you?" she asked and I figured it was somebody from school. She's such a sweet girl. Maybe if Nakia and I don't get back together then I can just be with her.

"Yes, but unfortunately I have a deadline so I need it now so I can register for fall classes." she said and after hearing that, I wanted to help her in any way that I could, but she would have to ask me first. Closed mouths don't get fed.

"Okay. Bye." she said and hung up the phone.

She sat back and folded her legs underneath her then began to pull at the sleeves of her sweater. All she had to do was ask me and her problems would be over. She got up and walked over to the door but didn't open it then walked into the kitchen. She came back with two beers and handed me one.

"I could use one and I just brought you one." she said and I nodded my head.

'Yeah I could definitely get used to this.' I thought to myself as I turned the bottle up. She'd had it open for me already so it was sweet on my end. I burped then smiled at her and sat my empty bottle down on the table. She picked it up then walked away.

"Kareem, listen." she began once she made it back into the living room. She stood directly in front of me and began to fidget nervously. "I'm sorry but I really needed the money for school."

I gave her a confused look as a warm feeling engulfed my body. I tried to sit up but it was like sitting up with someone sitting on your chest.

"What did you do?" I asked her as her front door opened.

My eyes widened in fear as I watched Pokey and Dread walk in smiling.

Miko

My mouth began to water as soon as I noticed that his dick was on hard. I knew he still wanted me but he just had that bitch in his ear. You know how them bitches be talking down on the next bitch. I bet that's what her lame ass been doing.

I began to get nervous all of a sudden as I thought about the fact that I fucked Christian and Casamoney today. I stared at Jaquan as he treaded slowly in my direction. I knew I needed to test the waters to see if I was back tight so I slipped my finger inside of me. A sigh of relief escaped my mouth because it was tight enough for Jaquan not to know that I'd gotten some earlier today.

Now before you judge me, don't act like you haven't had sex more than one time in a day. Just because I got it from different people don't matter. Hell, we all have fucked more than once. Let's just think about this as being round three. At least then it won't sound so bad.

I stood straight up and gripped my nipples tight in between my index finger and thumb as I stared at him. He licked his lips then walked right up to me and I was so excited. He slammed me against the wall hard and just when he was about to kiss me, his cell phone started ringing. He pulled it out of his pocket and when I saw Nakia's name flash across the screen I lost it. I snatched the phone out of his hand and slammed it into the ground as hard as I could. It bounced up and pieces flew everywhere.

"This is my time." I stated calmly as I reached out to him.

"Bitch it could have been important!" he slapped my hand away. "She can't find her fucking daughter and I was helping her!" he roared as he pushed me towards the door.

"Wait, I'm sorry!" I tried to explain as I fought my way back further into the house. I'd seen her daughter so I hoped that if I told him where she was that he would still give me some dick.

"GET THE FUCK OUT MIKO!" he screamed but I shook my head. I wanted this man like never before and I was going to get him back or my name isn't Miko Grey!

"I'm staying here with you!" I said sadly. "I need you Quan." I pleaded then dropped down to my knees. I knew that if my mom saw me at this very moment that she would shake her head at me just like I was doing on the inside.

"Naw man, it's over." he said as he grabbed my arm and pulled me back up to my feet. I jumped up and wrapped my legs around him to show him that I wasn't playing with him.

"I'm here to stay." I said as I bit his neck as hard as I could without drawing blood. I knew it would bruise and once he was around Nakia, she would think it was a hickey. That plus that phone call that I made will seal the deal for them.

Before he could say anything in response, his front door flew open and fell off of it's hinges. My mouth hung wide open and my heart jumped smooth out of it as I stared at my deranged fiance.

"What the fuck bruh?!" Jaquan yelled as he pushed me away from him again.

Christian didn't answer him because he was too busy staring at my naked body. There was no way that I could talk my way out of this, so I just stood there in all of my naked glory. Tears welled up in Christian's eye and I honestly couldn't believe that he was acting like this.

"I loved you." he said with a voice that was filled with hurt.

"And I love him!" I yelled and Jaquan looked at me crazy then shook his head.

Christian glared at both of us like he hated us with every breath in his body and I can't say that I blamed him.

"He doesn't love you." Christian said sadly as he held up a gun. I had no idea he knew how to use a gun. Sure I've seen it in his car, but I'd never seen it in his hands.

"Christian calm down." Jaquan said with his hands raised in the air. "It's not what you think." he continued and I just started crying. Yeah I wanted to be with Jaquan and I was willing to do anything for that to happen, except die.

"I'm sorry Christian. Baby you have to forgive me." I said then he pulled the trigger.

Sneak Peek! You won't believe what's next!!

Pregnant by my mother's husband
By: Bestselling Author Linette King

Jade

Beep.... Beep.... beep!

Wham! I swung my hand over to my nightstand and knocked the alarm clock over. It hit the floor with a loud thud but continued to beep. My failed attempt at hitting the snooze button caused me to have to get on up.

Well it was either get up or try to ignore the loud ass alarm clock that my dad bought me. See I'm not a morning person; and in my twenty years of living, I've never been one. I actually didn't plan on being one either, so opted to ignore the alarm.

"GET UP JADE!" my dad, Charles yelled from the living room.

I rolled my eyes and swung my legs over the side of the bed. My dad might as well be a drill Sergeant since he's up at the crack of dawn every morning. It really pisses me off too but I can't complain because I'm still under his roof.

Every morning at 5am my dad got up and made himself a healthy smoothie. The extra loud ass blender wakes me up but I always just go back to sleep. Each time I wished he would

155

just give me the money I needed to get my own place.

"Shit!" I cursed under my breath when I accidentally kicked the corner of my bed with my pinky toe.

There was no pain like the pain I felt at that very moment. I was convinced that there was nothing that hurt more than that in this world. Tears sprang to my eyes as I hopped around with one foot in my hands. My daddy opened my room door probably making sure I'd listened to him and got up but got an eyeful. It took everything in me not to laugh at him.

"Jade, baby what I tell you about sleeping naked?!" He fussed and closed the door with an attitude.

When the pain finally subsided, I smiled and shrugged my shoulders up like he was still at the door. Sleeping naked is literally the only control that I have here so I take full advantage of that. Everything that I do is controlled by him and I hate it!

I walked over to my full-length mirror and stared at my perfectly toned body. I've been working out since I was eighteen and you can definitely tell. I don't have a six pack because I don't want one, but my stomach is practically nonexistent.

I turned sideways and ran my hands over my perfectly round ass then slapped the bottom of my cheeks to make it bounce. I smiled as I cupped my small breast in my hand that are in fact so little that I don't have to wear a bra at all; so I don't unless I'm going to the gym. My dark brown skin was blemish free and my shape fit my 5'1" slim frame perfectly. I didn't have a boyfriend or anything because I was in love with myself. I literally looked at my naked body every day and got dressed slowly in the mirror.

Now, I'm not a virgin and I've actually been fucking this guy for about two years now; well on and off for two years. His name is Roni and I met him at the gym when I first started working out there; and I remember it like it was yesterday.

"Jade come here and let me talk to you for a minute." *my dad said as I sat in the living room of our house on the couch. I was all into this series I'd just started on Netflix called The Blacklist and I was just about to find out if Tom was really who he claimed to me.*

I reluctantly pressed paused and headed into the kitchen. For the life of me I couldn't figure out why he never came in the living room with me when it was time for these little talks. He always sat at the head of the kitchen table and I sat at the other end of it. The last time we had this talk it was because my mom wanted me to come stay with her for a few months. Of course I declined because you don't get to decide when you want me to be a part of your life, mother or not.

"Yes sir?" I said as soon as I sat down.

I needed us to get this conversation over with as soon as possible so I could get back to my show. It wasn't that I didn't like talking to my dad, it was just that sometimes I didn't want to talk to anyone.

"I love you Jade, but you graduated high school now and I'm not about to take care of someone not doing anything. I need you to set some goals and start working towards them. That's the only way you can stay here." he blurted out and my mouth fell open.

I graduated May 22nd and it's June the 1st! He's acting like I'm just leeching off of him or something. Hell, I'm still trying to figure out if I want to go to college or not. 'But he loves me.' I thought to myself as I rolled my eyes.

"Any goal?" I asked and he nodded his head not knowing I was about to get over on him. I knew he was serious but he knew that I'm the queen of loop holes. "I'm going to work on eating healthier. I'm gonna join the gym right now but I need to use the card."

I smiled as he shook his head and went into his wallet. He handed me his card, I grabbed my car keys and headed straight for Planet Fitness. I'd never been much of an active person and I had picked up a little weight, so this would help.

I walked into the gym with a purpose, signed up and got ready to leave until I caught a glimpse of the sexiest man I had ever seen in my life! He was tall, light skinned, had tattoos lining his arms and looked like his chest as well. He stood next to this girl and coached her as she worked out. The muscle shirt that he had on said Planet Fitness, so I knew he was one of the trainers here and I needed him to be mine. He's all the encouragement I needed to stick with this new goal that I'd set.

"Can I start now?" I asked the girl at the front desk and she nodded her head.

I smiled and made my way over to where he was training the heavyset girl and waited for him to look up at me.

"Good." he paused and looked at his watch. "Afternoon. I'm Tyrone, but you can call me Roni." he continued and extended his hand out to shake mine. It was sweaty but I still shook it with a smile on my face.

"I'm Jade and I need a trainer. I'm just starting out though and I want to tone everything up. I can come Tuesday's and Thursday's." I laid it on thick like I was really interested in just working out.

"That's cool, I'll be here. Are you in school or something?" he asked and I shook my head.
I notice his facial expression change just a little bit before he caught himself. I couldn't really read it, but I knew then that I needed to be in somebody's school to get somebody like him.

"I just graduated from high school. I don't start college until August." I half lied.

I hadn't even applied for college and I would sure be late and have to pay some type of late fee, but I knew my dad would love the news.

He smiled and nodded his head. He had the most beautiful teeth I'd ever seen. I wanted him and I wanted him bad, but I knew I had to play my cards right in order to get him.

"I'll see you tomorrow." he said since it was Monday. I smiled and headed home.

Knock.. Knock.. Knock..

The sound of my dad knocking on my room door snapped me back to the present. I quickly slipped on my underwear and bra.

"Come in." I said as I grabbed a graphic T shirt out of my drawer and pulled it over my head.

"Your class isn't until ten, right?" my dad asked as I slipped on a pair of jeans.

I nodded my head and glanced at my clock. It was only 7:15 but he insisted that I get up at 7 every morning. I purposely scheduled all of my classes so I could sleep in for the two years that I've been at the community college.

"Yes but I want to go to the library first and print out my paper." I lied because I really wanted to see if I could meet Roni before class since he's in town. My dad gave me the side eye and I knew it was because he tuned the extra bedroom into an office for us to share so I could print my paper in there. "We're out of ink," I said before he could ask me anything about it. We'd ran out of ink last week and I purposely didn't mention it because I knew I could use the fact that I was going to buy some to get out of the house.

"It's some in the closet in the room. Print your paper then I'm taking you out to eat breakfast before class." he said and I sighed heavily but didn't say anything to him. I simply nodded my head then walked past him and headed to the office. "I have someone I want you to meet." he said as he followed behind me.

I hoped it wasn't another one of the women that he'd been dating over the years. I've ran off about four of them because I knew that as soon as a woman got close to him, she'd make him put me out and I just wasn't going for that.
"Can't wait." I lied as I logged onto the computer.

This was going to be an extremely long day and I could already see that I would need a shot of something strong before it was over with.

Angela

I felt his hard dick press up against my ass and I already knew what time it was. At forty-five, I'd like to think that I still have it and I've got to considering the man that I'm married to is only thirty-eight and he can't keep his hands off of me.

I'm about 5'5" with caramel complexioned skin. I'm not in shape, but I'm not sloppy either. My ass sits up nice, round, and fat; but my titties droop a little bit so I always wear a bra. I have a little bit of gut but Tyrone makes me feel like it doesn't matter so I continue to eat what I want, when I want.

I moaned softly as I pushed back against his dick. He placed one arm around me and pulled me closer. His hot breath tickled the nape of my neck and I pushed back against him just a little bit harder. He slid one arm underneath me and grabbed my nipple. I moaned just a little bit louder to let him know that I liked what he was doing. He slid his other hand down my stomach and into my panties. I raised one leg slightly to give him access to my pussy. A sharp breath left my mouth as he found my clit and applied pressure to it. I circled my hips on his fingers with my ass pressed firmly against his dick. His breathing got heavier and I knew that he was ready to put it in.

I shimmied out of my panties then kicked them off of my bed. He raised one ass cheek and slid into me slowly. My breath got caught in my throat as I adjusted to his size. It had been about a week since the last time that we'd had sex because we've both been busy with work. Tyrone is a physical trainer and he contracts through different gyms so he can take his clients there. He makes great money doing that but I know it's because of his looks. A man that sexy will make any woman want to pay to be next to him, and that's exactly what they do. I don't care though because I know he would never cheat on me; and that's because he tells me all the time. He wants so much of me and then he's always worn out and doesn't want to do much else, so I know he's not giving it to anyone else. Plus I know how women are and if he was messing with anyone, they'd blow his phone up or something. His phone hardly ever rings if it's not a client and he leaves it around me. There's no way that he would leave his phone around me if he had someone else calling or texting him.

My eyes rolled to the back of my head when he began to pick up the pace. I knew he was ready to cum and wanted me to cum first. I arched my back so he could hit my spot just the way I needed him to.

"Ah, fuck! Harder!" I screamed out and he did as he was told.

He never made any noises during sex and after four years of marriage, I figured he was just the quiet type, so it no longer bothered me. I did enough screaming for the both of us.

"SHIT!" I yelled as I came all over his dick. He pulled out of me then rolled over onto his back. I put my leg down then laid on my back as well to give my side some rest. I'd slept on my left side then fucked on my left side and now my left leg was asleep.

"What time's your flight?" I asked as I wiggled my foot in order to wake my leg up. He smiled at me then rolled on top of me. I could feel his dick growing again but I'd just came and didn't care to go at it again.

"I have another hour baby." he said as he leaned down to kiss me. He raised my left leg and held it in the air with the bend of his elbow as he slid inside of me again. I inhaled deeply as he began to rotate his hips. "You know I love you, right?" he asked as he continued to slide in and out of me. I nodded my head because it felt so good that I couldn't speak. I closed my eyes and turned my head to the side as he worked his magic.

"You gone have my baby?" he asked and my eyes shot opened.

He knew how I felt about having children. I made that shit clear in the beginning that I had no interest in having any children at all. In fact, the thought of having a child dried my pussy up instantly and the dick was really hurting me.

"Move." I said as I gave him a light shove.

He frowned his face up but got off of me. I knew an argument that I didn't want to have was about to happen. I sat up in the bed and prepared myself for the verbal lashing that I was sure was about to come.

"You seriously don't want to have a kid with me?" he asked but it sounded more like a statement than a question. "Do you hear me talking to you?" he asked and I jumped slightly because he raised his voice an octave.

"Watch your tone be-"

"I ain't watching shit! What the fuck you marry me for Angie?!" he jumped up and asked.

I could see the vein in the neck sticking out as he screamed at me. I fell in love with him after only dating him for a few, but this conversation isn't news to him.

"Tyrone I told you from the beginning that I didn't want to have any children; so why you marry me?!" I matched his tone as I got on my knees in the bed. He walked away and started pacing the floor.

"What type of woman doesn't really want to have kids someday Ang?"

He sounded so defeated and honestly, my heart went out to him but damn, having children just isn't something that I wanted and he said he didn't want any as well.

"I'm sorry. I got my tubes tied and it's irreversible." I finally admitted and he just walked out of the room. I hopped out of the bed and followed him but I didn't say anything because I didn't know what to say to him.

"I'll call you when I land." he said as he grabbed his bags off the couch in the living room.

I sighed as I watched the love of my life walk out of the door. I'd let him down and there was no way that I could make it up to him. I just hoped he didn't leave me because of this.

I walked back to my room and hopped in the shower. I still had another hour before I had to open the store so I wanted to shower, get dressed, then go to the waffle house. I'm one of the store managers at Baber's and as much as I hated my job, I just couldn't afford to quit.

When Tyrone and I first got married, I was still living off of the money I'd taken from my last husband when I cleared our joint bank account. It was $25,000 and I figured if Tyrone and I put our money together, he'd end up spending mine; and I didn't want that. I told him that we should keep our money separate and it's been like that every since. He paid the rent and his car note, but I pay the utilities and my car note. That plus a shopping habit I developed when I was married to a man with money has drained my savings and I am now living from check to check.

I sighed heavily as I lathered my body with soap, rinsed off then climbed out of the shower. I should have stayed where I was but Tyrone provides something that my last husband never did, companionship. Sure Tyrone works a lot, but he always makes time for us. We still go out and we're still in love with one another. The only time I miss my ex-husband is when I want some money, but I have to wait until I get paid.

Sometimes I wonder how much money Tyrone has made but I don't know if I can ask him for any of it. Yes he's my husband but I've never opened the door for us to know what the other one is making. We never even borrow money from the other one and now I regret being selfish. I knew that if he decided to leave me, I'd have to move to an apartment because I wouldn't be able to afford to keep this house. I should have listened to my ex when he told me that I should buy a house with the money that I stole from him. At the time, I thought I'd be getting alimony and I wasn't expecting to have to go to work or save anything. I blew that money so fast but I have nothing to show for it. $25,000 gone and I'm renting a house I can't afford and paying notes on a car I can barely afford. I should have at least bought a car.

I got dressed in my work clothes then stopped in the kitchen. I debated on rather or not I should just cook me something to eat or go swipe this good ole credit card at the waffle house. Of course I decided to eat out. I had enough time to stop and grab something to eat, but I didn't have time to figure out how to cook grits. Shit just didn't come easy for me. I grew up with a mom who did everything for me and it ruined me. As old as I was I still fucked grits up, and definitely not in a good way. I enjoyed the mornings Tyrone would surprise me with breakfast because it was nothing like a good ole home cooked meal. Well, unless I was the one cooking it.

I shook my head, grabbed my keys and headed out of the door. I needed to mentally prepare myself for whatever it was that was about to happen in my life. I didn't know what it was but it was like I could feel the universe shifting underneath my feet.

Charles

I've had my daughter alone since she was eight years old, so that's twelve years of single parenting. I've tried to date here and there, but in my eyes a woman had to be accepted by my daughter as well. I've liked a few women enough to bring them around, but nobody could bond with Jade the way that I needed them to in order to be in my life. Then it dawned on me one day I was talking to one of my co-workers Charlene and she told me what the problem was.

"You're all she's got Charles." Charlene said. "You give her everything that she wants and you control every part of her life. She's grown now and if she was dating then she would be a little bit more open minded towards you dating."

I've been thinking about her words ever since she said them, but I didn't know how to talk to my daughter about dating. I mean how in the hell was I supposed to tell her that I wanted her to get a boyfriend so she could get out of my business? Wouldn't that be me still in her business? I was beyond confused but I started looking for her a man. When I told Charlene about my plans, she gave me her nephew's resume, literally. He has maintained a 4.0 grade point average since he started at FAMU and this is his last year there. She's twenty and twenty-three, so it's not that big of an age difference there.

I've treated Jade like a queen her whole life, so I knew she would settle for nothing short of the same treatment from whoever she decided to date; and I hoped Cornel would know how to treat her.

I waited patiently for Jade to finish printing her paper out so we could meet them for breakfast. Once she was finally done, we headed out of the door without a word. Now I'm really hard on her because I don't want her to ever need a man other than myself, so I was so happy when she decided to enroll in school. I paid for everything and all she had to do was show up and pass her classes. As far as I could tell, she was loving it and I loved the sudden drive that took off. She'd been going to school and working out religiously. When she graduated, I wanted her to go to a university and she didn't have to worry about a thing until she was finished with school. I didn't want her working because I knew it would be a distraction. For me it was either school or work, and I chose both. It was hard as trying to work two jobs and go to school, but I did it. I own property here in Florida that generates income, plus I'm an Executive branch manager so we're pretty well off.

Not to brag but I make about fifteen thousand a month from my properties alone. Whenever Jade finishes school, I'm going to show her the properties that I have built for her and let her decide what she wants to do to the inside and how much she wants to charge her residents. I just want my child to make it.

"Daddy are you introducing me to another woman?" she asked as I pulled out of the driveway.

I couldn't help but laugh at her spoiled ass because she did not want me with anybody. I am currently dating someone but I'm not ready for her to meet Jade yet. I'm going to follow Charlene's advice and get her occupied with someone first.

"No baby." I said to her with a slight laugh.

I didn't even want to tell her what I was really up to. She'd probably jump out of the car and run for the hills. I glanced over at her and she was playing a game on her phone.

"Uh huh." she said without looking up.

I didn't respond to her because I didn't want to end up giving the surprise away. I drove straight to Denny's, parked then got out of the car. She stayed seated like I knew she would until I made it around to her side of the car and opened her door for her.

"Thank you." she said as she placed her phone in her hand bag. She reached out to me so I could help her out of the car then together we made our way inside of the building.

"For two?" the hostess asked as soon as we walked in. I shook my head then held up four fingers. Jade shot me a look but knew better than to question me in front of anyone.

"One should already be here. Charlene?" She nodded her then grabbed two menus and lead us back to where Charlene was.

Charlene and I have been friends for about ten years so Jade already knows her and she loves her so much. She used to watch her for me while I worked a second job trying to get ahead so I could take care of her. I guess she's something like a God mom to her.

"Hey Ms. Charlene!" Jade said filled with excitement as she walked fast over to her.

Charlene stood up and embraced her then they both sat down. Jade started talking a mile a minute about school and working out. I could tell she was proud of herself and I was proud of her too.

"Ms. Charlene I'm so glad it's breakfast with you though!" Jade said after she'd finally taken a breath. I just shook my head and listened to her talk. "I thought he was trying to introduce me to another woman!" she said then wiped mock sweat from her forehead and Charlene laughed at her.

"Don't entertain her." I said as I looked between the two of them.

They got along so well and I just wished Jade had that relationship with her real mother.

The way she up and disappeared, you'd think she died or something.

Nope, Jade's mother is alive and well living somewhere in Alabama without a care in the world. Her mom left when she was eight. She just decided she didn't want to be a mother and I didn't try to stop her. I knew I could raise my daughter to be a much better woman than her mom ever could. Anyway, her mom didn't even reach out to me for her until she turned eighteen and even then, she didn't want her to come live with her; she wanted to come here for a weekend and catch up. The thought alone still pisses me off.

"Daddy I didn't mean to upset you." Jade said once she noticed my attitude.

Little did she know my attitude had nothing to do with her and everything to do with her dead beat ass mama. If I saw her, I'd tell her everything I've always wanted to tell her but didn't.
"It's ok baby I-"

"Our guest has arrived." Charlene cut me off, stood up and walked away.

Jade and I both turned to look. I figured the young man that she hugged was her nephew Cornel. I looked back at Jade and didn't like her facial expression at all. She had her mouth wide open and it gave me second thoughts about having her date someone just so I could. I suddenly realized the error I'd made by not allowing her to date sooner. I thought that if I treated her like a queen, she would only accept that but I could be wrong. What if he treats her like shit? Women loves a challenge, so she may try to give more of herself to him to get him to treat her better. I didn't want my baby to lose herself or forget what she's worth in order to please a man. My heart raced as they approached the table.

"This is Cornel." Charlene introduced us.

I grabbed his hand tight but he matched my squeeze. *'Shit, he ain't scared.'* I thought to myself as I sat back down. I zoned out when she introduced him to my daughter until she stood up and hugged him.

"Jade!" I called out astounded.

I was so out done at how easy she was behaving. I looked at Cornel and he looked nothing like his resume. He looked like he break hearts for sport and I would shoot his young ass if he ever hurt my child.

Jade blushed as she pulled away from him and sat down in her chair. I glared at them as they talked about a bunch of bullshit and Charlene shook her head at me the whole time. I couldn't wait for 9:30 to hit so we could get the hell out of here; but he offered to take her to class and she agreed.

"Let her live." Charlene said as I watched them walk away from the table still talking.

If I didn't know anything else, I knew what chemistry was and they had it. They clicked instantly and I didn't like it.

"I gotta go." I said as I tossed enough money on the table to cover everyone's food and walked away.

I didn't tell her bye or anything because I was truly pissed off. There's no way I expected for it to go that good for him, or for him to look like he was going to take advantage of my daughter. I should have thought this one out before I agreed to it. I was thinking selfishly and probably threw my baby girl out to wolves. I needed to speak with Sydney so she could calm my nerves down. Hopefully I didn't get one of those "I told you so's" because she'd definitely told me not to go through with it.

I headed out to my car and called her just to make sure she was available for me to come through and she was, so I headed straight to her house. I had the radio blasting, playing my all-time favorite songs by Sir Charles Jones. I nodded my head and sang along all the way to Sydney's house.

"Hey baby." she said as soon as I stepped out of the car.

She was standing outside in front of her door waiting on me when I pulled up. She wore sweat pants, a big t-shirt and gloves, so I knew that she was working in her garden when I called her.

"Hey yourself." I said to her as I walked up to her and gave her a kiss on her lips then walked inside of the house. I kicked my shoes off in her foyer and placed them by the door then waited for her to come inside.

"So how did it go?" she asked as she pulled her gloves off and placed them next to my shoes.

She then removed her shoes followed by every item of clothing and I knew it was because she didn't want to any dirt anywhere inside of her house.

"Great. I think she likes him." I answered as she passed by me.

She stopped and looked back at me with a smirk on her face. A small chuckle escaped her lips then she headed on down the hall to her bathroom.

"I knew you weren't ready for her to date. Y'all feel the same way about each other dating." she tossed over her shoulder as she walked in the bathroom and turned the shower on. I walked in and sat down on the toilet so we could talk as she showered.

"She thinks I'm going to write her off but I don't want her to get hurt; so we don't feel the same way Syd." I said with a voice filled with frustration that wasn't because of her. I was mad at myself for not listening to her.

"Baby you can't stop the pain that will come to her eventually. Things like that are just inevitable." she said then pulled the shower door open so I could join her. Without hesitation, I hopped in.

More than Friends
By: National Bestselling Author Envy Mayes

Chapter 1 (Shayla)

It was six o'clock in the morning as I stood in the bathroom mirror looking at a person I didn't even recognize anymore. It seemed like just yesterday, I was a beautiful, popular, happy go lucky captain of an amazing cheerleading team. I was so happy back then, but it was because I didn't have a care in the world. That was a little over ten years ago though, and I'm far from being that person.

As I stared at my reflection, I debated on rather or not I should call in to work. I didn't know if my eyes were swollen from me crying all night or from Simon punching me in my face. I shook my head at the sight before me.

"Oh my God!" I said as I turned my head to the side and saw a bruise that covered my whole cheek all the way up to my eye. "THAT MOTHERFUCKER!" I screamed at the top of my lungs.

I had to do something quick because I had to take my kids to school. I don't even know what set him off like that because he normally wasn't violent towards me.

We had been together since we were fifteen years old and moved in together right after graduation. We worked our asses off to pay for our fairy tale wedding when we turned twenty-one; then at twenty-three, we had our first daughter Samair. At twenty-six, we added our twin boys, Marko and Meeko to our clan. I guess that means it was safe to say that we knew each other well. He knew for a fact that him not bringing his ass home for the last two days was going to start some shit, but he obviously didn't care. Every time I called his phone, he kept telling me that him and Jayden were handling business at the club. I knew that a lie though because I'd drove by there and neither one of their cars were there. I can't speak for nobody else but I literally hated to be lied to. That's why as soon as he brought his lying ass through the door, I confronted him and was ready to fight.

He tried to brush me off and kept walking down the hall like he wasn't paying me no attention and that was something else that I hated. Don't ever ignore me! Ignoring me takes me to another level of crazy and he should know by now that that isn't what he wants to do!

I slapped the back of his head hard as hell because I was pissed beyond reasoning. He turned around and pushed me against the hallway wall.

"Shut up with that bullshit before you wake my kids up!" he spoke through gritted teeth.

I didn't think about none of that though. "You didn't give a damn about your kids when you was hanging your ass out in the streets for two days!" I shouted in his face. If they woke up oh fucking well because he was not about to treat me like this! "Simon I'm so tired of your shit! You act like you fucking Jayden as much time as y'all spend together!" I snapped and I was serious as hell. He turned around with a look of death in his eyes and punched me in the face.

To say that I was shocked would be an understatement because he'd never done anything like that before. He didn't even check to see if I was okay, apologize or nothing. He just grabbed some things out of the closet and left without saying a word.

I picked up the phone to call my best friend Tee so she could come get the kids and take them to school. I had to get to the bottom of this situation before something else happened. Simon had been acting out of character for a couple of months now. I guess it was time that I put him and whatever nappy head trick that he was messing with, in check with these hands.

I decided to clean up before I went to find my husband. Cleaning always helped calm me down and I knew that if I went to find him right now that I'd do something to him that I would regret. I was almost done cleaning when my message alert tone sounded on my phone. I knew his ass was going to be texting me before long but I didn't want a text message from him. I wanted to see him so I could talk to him face to face. I knew we should always keep our hands to ourselves but I didn't think that would happen. I walked into the living room to get my phone so I could see what he'd said.

"Damn, I guess I was wrong." I said out loud once I saw the message came from an unknown number.

I opened the message and my mouth hung open in disbelief. My heart dropped down into the pit of my stomach and I felt light headed. Nothing could have prepared me for what I saw. It was a video of Simon and Jayden being intimate, very intimate. Who am I kidding? I mean why am I trying to sugar coat what I'd saw with my own eyes for you? They were fucking! Fucking hard and it sickened me to watch the man that I loved getting hit from the back by his best friend. We've been together our whole lives and I honestly thought that I knew him, but I guess that I didn't. I fell back onto the couch as I tried to catch my breath.

"I'm going to kill both of them mother fuckers!" I said out loud as fresh tears stung my cheeks. I tried to think of a reason that I should let them live but I drew a blank. "They gone die today!" I said out loud as I hopped up.

I couldn't believe my husband did this to me and our children. I had been blowing up his phone for hours on end but I still couldn't get an answer. I paced the floor of my bedroom as I tried to figure out my next move. I wanted to kill them and I had even left, but I needed to be free for my children.

"Oh my gosh!" I screamed out loud as I threw my body on the floor.

I pulled my knees up to my chest and placed my head in the palms of my hands as visions of Simon and Jayden fucking flashed across my mind. I was literally sick to my stomach, but I was able to make it to the bathroom before I threw up; I just didn't make it to the toilet. Vomit splashed all over the floor and on the side of the tub but all I could do was cry. I knew I needed to clean it up, so I pulled myself together and started cleaning.

My phone buzzed again once I was done, but I was afraid to check the messages. It buzzed again, and again, and again. It buzzed so many times that I'd lost count. I made my way to my phone slowly and say that it was about ten pictures of him with other men. Some of the pictures were taken out of state.

"He's been taking them on trips?!" I asked myself in disbelief. "He never takes me anywhere!" I yelled with a voice filled with rage. I'd been knowing this man since we were fifteen years old, this had to be some type of prank.

Simon is one of the realest, hardest niggas that I know. There was no way that he'd be taking in the ass like a champ. If I hadn't seen it with my own eyes then I definitely wouldn't believe it. He'd betrayed me in a way that was unforgivable.

I knew I couldn't deal with this alone but I was too embarrassed and confused to call my girls. The sad part about this is, I didn't know if I wanted to leave him or not. I decided to go ahead and call them because I knew they would ride with me no matter what I chose to do. My hands shook like leaves on a tree during a windy day as I dialed Tee's number. I'm not a weak woman by far, but I couldn't hold back the tears that continued to roll down my face. On the third ring, Tee picked up the phone in her normal playful, proper voice.

"Hey boo, what's up with you?" she asked.

"Tee." I dragged out. "I need you." I continued with fresh, hot tears streaming down my cheeks. I could barely hold it together as I held the phone firmly to my ear.

"Shayla what's wrong? Are you hurt?" she asked in a worried tone. I knew I scared her with my sobs because she knows for me to be crying that he has to be something serious.

"Not physically." I answered her then started crying all over again.

"Hold on, let me get Tootie on the line." she said then I heard the phone click.

I knew she was going to call Tootie on three way so I could talk to them both at the same time. When she clicked back over, I could already hear Tootie's mouth. Tootie stayed ready so she never had to get ready, and that's why a slight smile came to my face when I heard talking about snatching some hoes off of their feet. That was the first time that I'd laughed since I saw that video of my husband and his best   friend.

"Naw not this time." I confessed sadly. I broke down as I told them all of the gory details about what I'd just found out. Even though I couldn't see their faces, I knew from the silence that their mouths were wide open.

"Oh my gosh Shayla I'm so sorry! What are you going to do?" Tee finally spoke up after a few moments of silence. My heart hurt so bad and all I wanted was for the pain to stop. I just didn't know how to stop it.

"I don't know." I answered honestly. "I was hoping you guys could help me sort this out." I continued although I didn't really know what we were supposed to be sorting out.

"If by sort it out you mean fuck him up then I'm all in." Tootie said and I believed her without a doubt. There's nobody on earth that that crazy heffa is scared of. She'll fight any woman big or small and will even go head up with a man.

"Try to calm down and I will be there in fifteen minutes." Tee said in a reassuring tone. It made me so happy that I called them.
"I'm coming too." Tootie chimed in.

By the time they got there, I was already drinking and smoking a blunt. I needed both of my stress relievers to help me through this ordeal that Simon put me in. I knew that if I didn't get fucked up, I'd end up killing him and going to jail.

"Hey bestie how are you holding up?" Tee asked but before I could respond, Tootie walked up on the porch dressed all black.

"From the looks of it, not too good." Tootie said as she made her way inside of the house. I couldn't even lie about how I was feeling, but I couldn't describe it either.

Once we got in the house, I showed them the video and that pictures that I'd received. I could heard Simon's moans as they listened to it and it hurt me to the core. I'd never felt this much pain in my entire life.

"I don't think I could ever forgive him for that Shayla." Tootie admitted. When I looked up at her, she was shaking her head and looking at me through sad eyes.

"Does he know about this?" Tee asked but I shook my head. Had he answered either one of my calls he would definitely know about it.

"No he is ignoring my phone calls because we had a fight this morning." I said as I subconsciously touched my face but the swelling had gone done a little.

"About what?" they asked in unison.

I thought back on the argument that we'd had and debated on rather or not I should tell them. *'What the hell?'* I thought to myself as I began to tell them everything that had happened.

The more that I thought about it, the angrier I got. I called Simon's phone one last time and he sent me to voicemail again. The wheels in my head began to turn and I figured he was probably somewhere fucking somebody's man. We hadn't had sex in two weeks and that's not like him because he has a high sex drive. I shook my head as I visualized him with all of those men in those pictures. *'If you can't trust your husband, who can you trust?'* I thought to myself as I gripped the phone tight in my hand.

I forwards the video and pictures to his phone so he'd see exactly what I saw.

"I'm going to find these cheating bastards." I said as I walked in my bedroom to change clothes. "I need you to drive your truck Tootie because they'd know our cars a mile away." I said to Tootie and she nodded her head.

"Are you sure about this Shayla?" Tee asked and I thought about it for a few seconds because I was about to go down a road that was only one way in and one way out.

"Very sure. Nobody plays with my heart without one helluva fight." I said and we walked out   of   the   door   together.

Chapter 2 (Simon)

Shayla has been blowing up my phone nonstop but I wasn't ready to talk to her just yet. It wasn't until she sent the video of me and Jayden that my heart damn near stopped beating and hopped right out of my chest.

"Shit!" I said as I stared at the screen. "Shit!" I screamed at the top of my lungs.

How is the hell did she get this? Who could have recorded this and knew to send it to her number? A million and one questions were running through my head. My main concern was my wife and kids though. I know I've been in these streets doing some foul shit but it was never supposed to go that far; and it damn sure wasn't supposed to make it back to Shayla. She's a beautiful, hard working woman and excellent mother to our children. She's crazy as hell though, and she ain't the forgiving type.

I didn't know what to do and to think. I put my hands on her for telling the truth. Shayla had never said anything like what she said this morning and it pissed me off so bad that I lost control. I guess it really is true what they say, the   truth   hurts.

If you had ever told me I would fall in love with a man, I would have beat the brakes off of you. I hated homosexuality, but I guess it was because I never understood it. I love women too though. All kinds of women and I'd banged plenty of women in my day, but this was totally different. Jayden and I grew up together and were business partners for a few years. I owned two strip clubs, a tattoo shop and a barber shop, so financially my family was straight. I'm just not sure how straight I'm going to be when Shayla finally catches up with either of us. I wanted to call and explain or text her and say I'm sorry for hurting her. I wanted to tell her that I was drunk and rolling off of X when Jayden took advantage of the situation, but what would be my reason for continuing it for the last four months if I didn't like it or want it. I quickly changed my mind and called Jayden instead. He answered immediately.

"What's up bruh?" I could tell he was in a good mood because he sounded real chill.

"Everything nigga. We need to meet now at the spot!" I told him pissed off. I couldn't believe that shit had finally gotten back to Shayla but I guess everything done in the dark will definitely come to the light.

"At the spot huh?" Jayden asked in a jealous tone of voice. The spot was an apartment I had rented for a stripper that I was fucking with last year but it went south and I sent her ass north. "Whatever is going on, if you can't tell me on the phone it's going to have to wait." he continued.

"And why is that?" I asked as I tried to remain calm but it wasn't working because my temples were throbbing.

"Today is family day and me and your sister is out with the kids."

"That's right bruh, family first." my sister added in the background. "You should be at home with yours. Y'all always working but us wives need our time too." she continued as she laughed in the phone.

I gave a fake ass chuckle. "Yeah you right sis. Let me speak back to that man of yours right quick."

"Okay big bruh. I love you." she responded then put Jayden back on the phone.

"Nigga you better have your ass at club Envy tonight or that happy little family man you playing will be dead." I snapped because nobody is going to put me on the backburner for no fucking body. He got me fucked up.

I turned to get something off of my desk and I caught a glimpse at the security camera in the lobby. Sure enough it was Shayla, Tee and Tootie and by the looks on their faces, Shayla had exposed my secret and they were here for revenge. Three minutes later Shayla was banging on the office door.

"Simon I know you in there, so open the door and talk to me." she said but I didn't make a move for the door. "So you gay now motherfucker?!" she screamed after several seconds of just standing there.

Boom! Boom!

They all began to kick the door hard as hell. I was speechless because just hearing her say that made me feel like a monster. My intentions were never to hurt her and the shit with Jayden just kind of happened.

I listened to my wife go from screaming to crying to asking me over and over again

"Why?" I didn't have a answer for her because I still didn't know why.

"Shayla go home and calm down please. We can talk about this later." I said to her without opening the door.

"Open this door and face me like a man Simon!"

The more she cried, the more I wanted to open the door and hold her, but I knew better. If I opened that door, her and her friends were going to jump on me. I know them and I have seen them in action; and I couldn't handle all of them together without hurting one of them and that would be another problem.

"Let's meet baby and talk by ourselves when you calm down some; because I know you been drinking and not thinking straight. It's not what you think, I promise." I lied because we both knew that it was exactly what she thought. Pictures don't lie and a video damn sure don't.

"I'm going to get you for this Simon! You got me and my kids fucked up and tell Jayden too! I'm about to crumble y'all world." she threatened and I believed every word.

A few minutes later, I watched them exit the club on surveillance cameras. I breathed a sigh of relief because that was a really close call. I wondered what she had planned for us thought because I knew it wasn't going to be anything good. Her family is associated with some very powerful people. Not only that, but she knew a lot about Jayden and I; and some of her family members are cool with ours. I hope she didn't hurt my sister though.

'I need to get somewhere to stay until this boils down.' I thought to myself as I picked up my keys. I guess I'll get a hotel room so I can shower and get back to work. I decided to go out the back so I could see around the front before getting   in   my   truck.

The coast was clear so I proceeded to my truck. When I got close up on it, it was destroyed. All the windows on my Land Rover were busted out, my tires were slashed and it had all kind of gay obscenities sprayed painted all over it.

"What the fuck!" I said out loud as I shook my head.

That bitch is really crazy. I knew I messed up but she didn't have to do all of this to my car.

CPSIA information can be obtained
at www.ICGtesting.com
Printed in the USA
LVOW03s0109141117
556123LV00020B/806/P